The Waiting Room

ALYSHA KAYE

The Waiting Room

Copyright © 2014 Alysha Kaye

To Gardner.
To the people who have waited
and the people who have not,
for both have equally shaped my
today and tomorrow.

www.alyshakaye.com

alyshakaye7

Alysha Kaye, Author

CHAPTER 1

I didn't know it at the time, but I was waiting.

"Why are you still here, man?"

Everyone was staring. Some simply amused or curious, some with amazed mouths open, some with suspicious eyes, and others with pure envy. I didn't know why the hell I was still there. But I was definitely regretting telling this man that I'd been here for over half a day. Most people didn't give two shits about me; everyone just ignored each other actually. But when I told this guy how long I'd been in here, he started spreading the word and now, apparently, I was some sort of spectacle.

"Hey man, I said *why* are you still here?"

I was too busy watching Nina. She was lying in our bed, staring at the ceiling, wrapped in nothing but my holiest white undershirt. She looked beautiful, hair tangled in black mobs around her, her eyes were always more green than brown when she cried.

I snapped out of it when the guy shoved me.

"I SAID WHY THE HELL ARE YOU STILL HERE?"

His whole body was shaking. "I LOVE MY WIFE TOO GODDAMNIT!" He was yelling at the receptionist now. I just went back to watching Nina. She had moved her arm from over her chest to behind her pillow.

"Mr. Pierre, I understand, but there's nothing we can do. You have about two minutes now. I'm sorry."

His shouting turned to sobs. I could feel more eyes than before burning into me from every angle.

"Johanna and Fernando Alvarado!" The receptionist made a check on a clipboard as a round-faced pregnant woman was led out the side door.

Nina rolled onto her stomach. I wanted to kiss the arch of her foot, the skin behind her knees. It suddenly hit me. I forced myself to turn away and walked over to the balding man lying in a ball on the floor.

"I don't understand." I stared at the tears soaking into his mustache.

"Are you an idiot?" He glared up at me. "You get to wait."

As I opened my mouth to ask *Wait for what?* the receptionist called, "Luis Pierre!"

He stood, slowly, and brushed off his gray slacks even though they were pristine. "Lucky bastard," he muttered, leaving me to gaze after him in complete bewilderment. Looking back, I wonder how he knew. I guess he just figured, what else would I be doing, waiting there for so long.

I stumbled over to the tiny gray-haired receptionist. Her body looked like a 12-year-old, her face like an 80-year-old. The name tag on her white button-up read "Ruth."

A red-haired woman who was clutching the arm of a

chubby, red-haired little boy was leaning across the desk. I caught the end of her question, "...any way I can find him?"

"No ma'am, I'm afraid not. Yes, Mr. Floyd?" Ruth looked at me expectantly. The red-haired woman drew her son in closer to her hip and whispered, "How do you do it?" I looked from her to Ruth, Ruth to her.

"Um." I craned my neck to see if I could see Nina from here. I couldn't. I started to get anxious.

"Mrs. Stevens, may I ask you to please sit back down? Mr. Floyd is new." Ruth sounded one tone away from robotic. Yet comforting. An understanding robot.

"Oh." The woman looked at me the way I would look at a cross between an elephant and a Chihuahua. She walked away, her son peering back to stick his tongue out at me.

"Mr. Floyd, I'm sorry no one has spoken with you yet. It's a really busy time of year. Why don't you take this packet? I'm guessing you need the English version?" Ruth handed me a thick, stapled stack of paper and then called out, "Diana Peng!" I couldn't help but notice the look she tried to hide—fighting to stay professional. I was apparently a freak.

Everything reminded me of Nina. Our freshman year of college when I went with her to buy a pregnancy test (false alarm). Junior year when the health club was raising STD awareness and Nina forced me to get tested with her (also a negative, in case you were wondering). Strange that this place obviously had a hospital-esque vibe. Definitely not my idea of heaven, which is where I thought I was when I appeared in this bright room. But there are no clouds or angels playing harps.

To be honest, I didn't expect anything to happen after death. I expected them to scrape my body off the highway and wrap it up in a sheet, to later be shoved into a box, which would then be tossed into the earth. Simple really, like gardening. But somehow my body wound up here, unscathed, same clean work clothes, tie straight. I closed my eyes behind the wheel of my Jetta and when I opened them, I was standing in front of a large window watching the aforementioned scraping process. So my body's in two places? I don't know. I don't feel like a "soul." What is a soul? Who even says we have one? Everyone thinks they'll have the answers after they die, but apparently, you just get more questions.

One Week Ago…

I walked inside to the smell of spaghetti and garlic toast, one of the few meals Nina can cook well. My nose led me into the kitchen. I don't care that she cooks it every Tuesday or that the guys at the office make fun of me for bringing the leftovers every Wednesday. She's been making it for a decade and I think my body would shut down or something if I didn't have it as often.

"Hey Booger, how was work?" She smiled and stirred the noodles a bit.

I noticed a spot of sauce on her bottom lip and I was quick to kiss it off. "Eh, it was alright. As good as the financial planning world could be." I kicked off my slacks and hung them on a kitchen chair.

"Babe, I wish you'd do something you love. You're not an old man. It's not too late to do something crazy." She held out a piece of turkey meat on a wooden spoon.

"I've told you so many times, we spent our entire 20s being dirt poor. I don't want to put you through that again. You teach high school English, baby; your salary won't exactly hold us."

"Put me through what exactly? You know that was the most fun we've ever had. We did everything we've ever really wanted to do. We travelled across Europe for God's sake. We lived in NYC for two years. It was bliss." I noticed another sauce spot on her shirt.

"But we're gonna start trying to have a baby soon."

"Oh, are we?" She grinned.

"We *are* 30, Nina." That's what we'd always said. That was the magic number.

"I guess my uterus is ready."

And we microwaved the spaghetti later.

I was back in front of my window now thinking, shouldn't this room be a lot bigger? People die every minute, yet there's only about 50 people milling around. Some reading magazines in the leather airport-looking chairs. No one looked confused, like me. What were we all waiting for? A private meet-and-greet with God/Satan? Our journey to the Golden Gate/fiery depths of Hell?

Nina was finally asleep, I could relax. We'd always

promised that when our wrinkles sagged across the surface of every one of our limbs, we'd find a way to say sayonara to the world together. We contemplated a hot air balloon ride gone wrong, popping pills, a dramatic plane crash (me being the pilot of course)...so obviously, I was worried that she would try to catch up with my unexpected departure. But so far, just a lot of sleep, a lot of avoiding people, food, and showering. I was too early. I left her—her worst fear.

I'd sat at the window for a whole day. People were making funeral arrangements. And I had a packet in my lap that would hopefully explain why my name wasn't being called by Ruth. Maybe nobody wanted me. Maybe I was getting to return to life, like Bruce Almighty. I watched Nina breathing for a little bit longer until I felt like I was lying next to her, her breath hitting my ear softly. Then I turned over the first blank page.

Hate to inform you that you're dead...blah, blah, blah (skimming)...Out your window you'll see...blah, blah, blah (yeah, I got it)...Your Exit (ah-hah! I'm guessing this is the right section).

After arrival, your name(s) will be called shortly. As your name(s) is/are called, please exit through the side door. You will have no recollection of this room until your next visit.

My reading was interrupted by a really young guy, maybe 19 or 20, abruptly sitting down right next to me (everyone was pretty spread out). He smelled like weed (he smelled like high school).

"So what have you figured out so far?" He winked and

nodded towards the packet in my lap.

"Um…" Did this kid work here or something? Is it possible to have a job after you bite the dust? Ruth obviously works here. Or is she not dead?

"You're a newb, right?" He flicked his sandy bangs out of his eyes and grinned.

"Sorry, what?" Christ, I'm old. And I really shouldn't even be *thinking* the Lord's name in vain in a place like this. Never too late to be saved, right?

"Your first time here?" He pushed his aviators down from the top of his head to the tip of his nose.

"Oh. Yeah. That obvious?"

"Just a little. If old Ruthie's not helpin' you out much, I'm a pro around here." He laughed, a loud and short burst. So this was my savior? I was briefly reminded of the song, "What if God was One of Us?"

"Jude Floyd." Might as well get comfortable with the kid.

"The Beatles, nice dude. Jake Reynolds." He grabbed my hand, didn't quite shake it, and slumped farther down into his chair. "So seriously, what do you know?"

"Well, we're dead for one." I tossed the packet aside as he let out another quick burst of laughter. "Everyone leaves pretty quickly after getting here, anywhere from 20 minutes to an hour. Except me, which people do not seem to be pleased about."

"Listen, people read the packet, they know the packet, but they still have hope. Human flaw I guess. Not your fault. They're probably just having trouble placing you." What the hell was he talking about? He leaned forward, elbows on knees. I did the same.

"Placing me?"

He sighed. "Ever heard of reincarnation?"

Oh shit. "Sure."

"Well that's a fancy version of what really happens. This is my tenth life."

"Are you telling me I've been waiting here for five hours to get turned into a plant or a cat or something?"

"Five, really? Wow. And fuck no, this is a strictly human-to-human operation."

"So what you said about people having hope…"

"Well, you know, most people want to be with someone specific for all of their existence. But the packet says what the packet says. They're just in denial."

"Nina." Slowly, the pieces were coming together.

"That your girl?"

"My wife."

He saw the glint in my eye. "Well look dude, I'm sure you love her and all that, but you won't remember her one bit after you walk through that door. A new woman every life. It's pretty awesome. And when you come back to the waiting room, AKA when you die again, you get to chill as whatever life you liked best, AKA Jake Reynolds. Good times, man."

Way too many questions were begging to be let out, but I asked the one I was most curious about. "Why do some people take longer than others?"

"Lemme put it this way—even though you won't remember your past lives while you're living another, you're still in there. In the body, I mean. It's just new skin, you know? The 'you' inside has to fit your surroundings I guess. But shit, I haven't been in California every time, so I guess that's just a theory." Yet another short cackle.

"So this packet doesn't tell you all that stuff?" I felt like I was shaking, but I wasn't.

"Hell no. Well, I mean, yeah, but not in those words. They gotta keep it interesting I guess. It does explain how there are like, a billion of these rooms. Makes sense." His dimples remained permanently.

I was starting to get annoyed. "So every time you come back here, you remember *all* of your lives?"

"Yup. Every little detail. Kind of makes my head wanna explode sometimes."

"So every time, you wind up in a different waiting room or what?"

"No, no. This is my home base. ISN'T THAT RIGHT RUTHIE BABY?"

"But how do you know which life you liked best?"

He took off his aviators and gave me an *Are you serious* look. "Dude…you just know. I mean, look at me. This was obviously my most attractive life. AKA the hottest girls, AKA the hottest memories."

I couldn't imagine having a happier life than the one I had with Nina. Unless it's a longer life with Nina.

"Jake Reynolds!" We both looked behind us at Ruth, who gave Jake an exasperated raise of her eyebrows. He just laughed more.

"Maybe I'll see you around, buddy. Good luck, newb!" He clapped me on the back and made his grand exit, blowing "old Ruthie" a kiss before diving, yes, literally diving through the side door.

This was ridiculous. I walked over to the desk, checking on Nina first (still sleeping, on her side now).

"Mr. Floyd, did you read your packet already?"

"No, Ruth, I'd much rather talk to you. Plus, the packet doesn't explain why I've been here 10 times longer than all these people. I just learned more from a 500-year-old, yet underage, surfer than this shit." I slammed the papers onto the counter and tried to lower my heart rate. I don't usually get "bothered." I'm extremely placid. Nina calls me Jude the Nude sometimes because she thinks all nudists are relaxed hippies.

"Be that as it may," I'd told her the first time she explained her stereotype, "I hate being naked. So that just won't do as a nickname."

"You don't hate being naked with me." She gave me the *Let's be late to work* look. I love that look.

Ruth bit her lip and whispered, "Mr. Floyd, if I knew why you were still here, I would have told you hours ago. I'm sorry."

"But you realize what everyone thinks, right?" I softened my voice.

"That you're waiting." She looked down.

"Not waiting for my name to be called."

She gave up. "Waiting on her."

"Exactly. And I've decided, why not? Who cares what the damn packet says? So if anybody asks, yes, that is what I'm doing. I'm waiting on my wife."

I walked away, back to my window, ignoring the stares and gapes. Nina was waking up.

Four Days Ago...

"Your eyes are like the Atlantic and Pacific." Nina rubbed my eyebrows with her thumbs, as if she were trying to lay them down flat. She always did that in the mornings.

"Oceans..." I muttered, still half-asleep.

"Yeah, oceans. I hope our kids get them." She nuzzled into my chest.

"I like your eyes." I stretched.

"Boring, poop brown." She kissed my nipple.

"Well I hope they get your everything else then." I rolled on top of her, licking her shoulders, neck...

"MR. FLOYD! MR. FLOYD!" Someone was tapping me with those god-awful plastic nails, *hard*. I opened my oceans and unstuck my forehead from the glass. It was just Ruth.

"I was having a really good dream." I squinted up at her and then glanced down at Nina. Before I fell asleep, she'd been crying in the bathtub. Now she was back in bed.

"Yes well, I'm sorry. No one has ever slept in here." She put her hand on my hip and shook her head, like I was a science experiment gone wrong.

"Yeah, I thought heaven was supposed to rid you of hunger, thirst, all those earthly pains."

"This is not heaven, Mr. Floyd. And I take it you'd like

some lunch?"

My stomach growled loudly. "Is there a special of the day? Holy Hamburger? Mary Meatloaf? Angel hair pasta?"

"Very funny. Come with me."

I looked uneasily out the window.

"She'll be fine." Ruth once again gave away with her eyes that I was like a Ripley's Believe It or Not showcase.

"I'll be right back," I whispered to the glare of the glass.

Ruth walked me behind her desk and through a door that I had never noticed. A break room?

"Are you dead?" Might as well be blunt.

"No." Her whole body tensed, but she didn't hesitate with her answer.

"So this is literally your job? What do you tell people? How did you apply, was it listed on Monster?"

"I tell people the truth, Mr. Floyd, that I am an administrative assistant."

"Yeah, to God!" I was gaping. She glanced at me with pity and then opened a fridge and pulled out a brown bag. "I mean, that's your boss, right? Seriously, how did you swing this? Are you a nun?" I was no longer hungry, this was way too fascinating.

"Look Mr. Floyd—"

"Please call me Jude."

"Look Jude, I am not a therapist, I am not a babysitter, and I am not a nun. I do not need to answer any questions; I do not even need to be feeding you. I gave you a packet. You obviously haven't read it. From now on, here's the break room. Please clean up after yourself. However, I'm sure you won't be with us much longer." Her voice finally sounded less robotic. She slammed the brown bag on a table and crossed her arms.

"I'm sorry if I upset you Ruth, but I just want to know more about this place."

She sighed deeply. "This is The Waiting Room, what else is there to know?"

"Plenty. I'll start with: is this really a reincarnation factory?" I peeked inside the brown bag. An apple and a tuna sandwich. I would've preferred the Holy Hamburger.

"Mr. Floyd, I need to get back to the desk. I'm sure there are at least ten names that are ready by now. Plus, my shift's almost over. Maybe you'll find Joe more helpful."

"Jude. And can I take this into the almighty waiting room?"

"No, *Jude*, people will gawk."

"People are already gawking, Ruth!"

"Must I really bicker with you, Mr. Floyd? You must follow the rules here, understood?"

"Are you sure you're not a nun?" She threw her hands up and stormed back to her desk while I took about 30 seconds to scarf down the sandwich, shove the apple in my pocket, and get back to Nina.

Two Days Ago...

"I did it." I came rushing into the living room, where Nina was grading Hamlet papers and eating Hamburger Helper.

"Did what, Booger?" Her voice trailed off, she was deep into Red Pen World.

"Nina, listen. I did it! I took out a small business loan today at work. We're gonna create a new town."

"That's amazing! What shall you build first?" She kissed me long and hard before I could answer. I breathed in her perfume.

"Well the loan is actually enough to get started on a small movie theater—my favorite."

"Babe, are you serious? This is so great! Even though I'd rather you start with a decent pizza shop!"

We had moved to one of the smallest cities in Texas—it contained a Dairy Queen and a Dairy Queen parking lot. But teaching jobs were scarce and Nina jumped on the chance. Plus, Austin wasn't very far away, so I was able to find a boring bank job easily. But we were tired of driving for 30 minutes every time we wanted to go on a date. Most of the time, we just stayed in, dreaming up things we'd build right around the corner if we had the time and money.

We cuddled on the couch and finished off the stroganoff while I rambled on and on about starting my own business. It was all I ever wanted to do. The only question: when to quit my job.

"I shouldn't even be helping people with their finances. I'm not even good at it! Look at me, about to open my first business while simultaneously trying to impregnate my wife. I'm the one that needs advice."

Nina giggled and kept scratching my back. "Stop worrying, Honey. If you want, I'll start taking my birth control again…it's only been a few days."

"No! I want a mini mixture of us running around here.

I want more than one. I'll just make sure my businesses succeed. Small feat."

"Have I ever told you that I love you more than all the eyelashes in the world?" She was so random sometimes.

"You're never out of new ones, are you?" I brushed her bangs away from her eyes, but they soon fell back into place.

"You should try it, it's very satisfying."

"Alright. I love you more than all the freckles in the world." I'm not very original, she was the poet. But hey, I thought it was cute.

"Weak."

"Oh c'mon, everyone knows there's more freckles than eyelashes in the world."

"Are you kidding me? There are millions of people who don't have one single freckle."

"Yeah but then there are other people covered in them."

"But it doesn't matter because *everyone* has eyelashes."

"That is false. Besides, have you ever counted your eyelashes? Not that many."

"Have you ever counted your freckles? You have way more eyelashes."

She was probably right, but I thought I was fighting a fair fight. "Are you forgetting about the ones on my butt?"

"No, those are my favorite."

She smiled that smile where the creases of her mouth formed fake dimples. I loved those. She always said her body tried so hard to produce something she had always wanted. I told her one day that dimples weren't that special, that in Chemistry, we learned they were actually a dominant trait. She didn't care. She got pissed, ranting about how she *would* have a boring recessive gene.

I probably would've come up with something better than freckles if I would have known. I would've done a lot of things.

"You must be Joe." I stuck out my hand. Ruth had finally left (strange to think we'd actually be friends one day) and an extremely hairy, middle-aged man had replaced her.

"And you must be Jude." He smiled to reveal a mouthful of braces.

"I don't know why I'm surprised that you already know my name."

"Yeah, you're creating quite the stir. But hey, who wants to live a boring life, right?" He followed that one with a roar of laughter, turning the almost visible skin under his thick black hair bright pink. "Too soon?"

"Nah, I don't mind death jokes. But I promise I'll laugh next time if you help me out."

"What do you want to know?" He folded his hands over his protruding belly. "Debbie Tennant!" A tall, beautiful black woman strutted through the ominous door in red high heels.

"Seriously? That easy?"

"Well you've almost been here an entire day. I figure you're doin' just what everyone thinks you're doin'. Might as well let you in on the biz if you're gonna be here awhile."

"Wow. Ok. Thanks." I was dumbfounded. He was

nothing like Ruth.

"Ruth was that hard on you, huh?"

"Well I guess she's just trying to do her job."

"Yeah well, she's been here since the beginning. Never seen anything like you. I think she's just worried."

"How is it possible that she's been here 'since the beginning' if she's still alive? She told me she was alive."

"Well one thing I can't tell ya is someone's personal stuff. I might as well just give you her file!" Another loud roar of laughter. "La Shawn Stewart!"

"So are you alive too then?"

"You bet your ass I am. Different this time though. I'm a happy man now."

"What do you mean?"

Joe sighed. "I stuck a rifle under my chin about ten years ago, but I was given a second chance to live a better life, do better things. Paul Foster! So I woke up in my apartment, holding my rifle and my new work schedule for this old place. Best thing that ever happened to me."

"Wow. So this is some kind of redemption for you guys?"

"Nah, it's not like that for all of us. Like I said, I can only tell ya what I can tell ya."

"So who'd you talk to? When you died…"

Loud roar of laughter. "Ruth. She told me that I needed to 'get my act together'."

"So you came here?"

"Yup. I made my decision and she handed me a nametag and a schedule."

"So what if you would've chosen to…stay dead?"

"I woulda been sent to another life, endin' in the same

way."

"Who would ever choose *that*?"

"Most people don't wanna wake up in the same body, in the same apartment, with the same feelin' in their gut."

"Hmm." That was a lot to take in. But I was determined to squeeze as much information out of this guy as possible. "So the billions of people on Earth, they're just the exact same billions that have been living since the beginning of time?"

"Well, some of 'em. You're new, obviously. That damn population rate. Keeps gettin' higher. People like baby-makin' and I don't blame 'em." This man laughed more than anyone I'd ever met. I would've loved meeting him while I was alive. Probably at a sports bar. But right now, I just needed answers.

"So once you're...created or whatever, you just keep living lives, century after century...forever?" I had a brief picture in my head of an old TV show I used to watch with my dad—"Highlander", starring Duncan MacLeod, the centuries-old, sword-fighting badass who could only be killed if you chopped his head off and took all his powers.

"Well it's not that simple." He made kind of a wincing face. "You could wind up anywhere. I mean, in any time. It's, uh, kind of hard to explain. The packet explains better than I can."

"Are you saying that your lives aren't in chronological order?"

"Exactly. I have no personal experience since I'm, ya know, in one of my lives right now. But I'm sure I've lived in plenty of places and years...or maybe this was my first life, who knows."

"Right…since you only remember when you're in this…place." I rubbed my temples. College was a piece of cake compared to this "lesson."

"When you're in this place because you're dead, not because you're at work. You're gettin' it!" He picked at something in his braces.

"I've seen a ton of movies, Joe. But how can you physically, actually, *be reborn* in the *past*?"

"Hell if I know, buddy! That's just how it works I guess. The packet says it's a 'continuous cycle'."

The thought of being born before 1980 was not appealing to me. At all. Nina would be happy though. She loved the fashion and the language and the simplicity of the past. "You gonna be here awhile, Joe?"

"Yesiree. A full eight hour shift."

"I'll be right back."

Nina was still in bed. Her mom was sitting on the edge.

"We were trying to have a baby Mom." Now they were both crying. I felt the need to look away, but I couldn't. It was like our infamous need to stare at a car crash. But I caused this crash.

I watched Rose stroke Nina's head, brush her hair away from her face, rub her back…and I felt my eyes drooping.

Yesterday…

We finally rolled out of bed and said goodbye. I only pecked her lips, thinking how late I already was for work.

But she understood. She didn't like it when I messed up her vanilla lip gloss anyway.

What 30-year-old still wears vanilla lip gloss? She'd punch me and say "This 30-year-old."

She waved out of the doorframe as I sped down the highway and the next time I'd see her wouldn't be in fake dimples and sticky kisses. I only ever saw a work email, opened on my phone, and then an 18-wheeler for a quick second, as I was sliding into it. And then darkness. And then the bright waiting room. And then her again, through a window, untouchable.

They said she didn't need to identify the body, that they used my teeth or something. How CSI right? All they really mean is that the body's too messed up and they don't want her going psycho. As if seeing me would've made it harder than it already was. As if she already didn't have a picture in her head of what I looked like. She had seen blood, it was hard to miss. So what would've been the difference? But I guess I'm just saying that. I'm glad they didn't let her see me. She probably *would* have gone psycho. Trying to piece me back together or something. She didn't even believe them when they said I was dead.

I kept on thinking about time and how it all matters. The cliché, *what if I would have been with her for five more minutes?* Then I would've been on the highway five minutes later, and then there'd be no wreck. Or I'd be stuck in traffic because of a wreck killing somebody else's husband. But seriously, what if I would've kissed her goodbye one more time? A long, 30-second kiss. Taking off all of her Bath and Body Works "Cake Icing." Would that have made a difference?

Someone had taken my shoes and placed them neatly by a police car. How strange.

"Ma'am, I think it's time you head home." Some officer gripped her shoulder. I glared at his wedding ring creasing her shirt.

She was hugging the black dress shoes.

"Did you hear me, ma'am?"

She glanced at the 52 card pickup of "Jessie the Jetta." She always had to name my cars. And then she headed home to curl up in bed, surrounded by everything we had taken so long to build together.

A year and a half later, she took the shoes off her desk and put them in a box in our closet with all of our pictures. I forgot to take the sticker off the left one, she did that for me. It was dirty and faded, $44.99 Size 10.5. Later, she took the sticker out of the trash and smoothed it back on the bottom of the heel. One of the corners refused to stick, curling up, no matter how many times she laid it flat. She kissed it over and over for hours, tears soaking into every inch of leather.

CHAPTER 2

I watched Nina open the movie theater. She could have cancelled the small business loan under the circumstances, but she didn't. She quit teaching for a very long time. She opened the business, right around the corner, making everything just as I'd talked about. She waited for it to make just enough to pay off the loan and then she sold it.

I watched her take a pregnancy test even though she knew she wasn't pregnant. I watched her cry all the time.

Joe and I were quickly becoming good friends. We'd play poker at his desk and he'd let me call out names sometimes. We figured out that it was best if people thought I worked there too.

Best of all, he really had told me everything he could. Was there a God? He thought so. So this wasn't some alien experiment? "Hell no, boy! You one of those UFO creeps?"

I told him I was more likely to believe in aliens than God. What kind of God never showed himself? Never allowed you to die peacefully, go to a heaven?

"Well duh, this is the best kind of heaven. He's lettin'

us live forever. Immortality. Second chances. That *is* Him showin' Himself."

That was Joe's take at least. I wasn't buying it.

I watched Nina slowly begin to smile again. I've never wanted something so much and hated myself for wanting it even more. But I wanted her to join me. I was lonely and trapped.

"Joe, I don't get it. You get paid for this, right? Who signs your check?"

"It's cash. Waitin' for me every Friday here at the desk."

I wanted to know how much but I refrained from asking.

"This shit just doesn't make any sense." I tossed a handbook on the desk. I'd memorized every page, hoping to actually learn something. There was nothing. Nothing useful.

"Sorry, buddy. You can borrow my bible any time!"

"Shut up, Joe."

"Well it just so happens that I can oblige. It's two, my friend."

His 5:00 PM-2:00 AM schedule wasn't the best. I wanted to sleep as much as possible during Ruth's shift but that was when Nina was up. So I had to settle on sleeping from 2:00 AM to 8:00 AM, Tara's shift, which also wasn't the best because she was honest with me, which I loved. Quite eccentric though, not really my cup of tea. Nonetheless, I quickly began to feel like her big brother. She was only 18!

"J, why can't you just deal with the fact that this place is just like everything else? Who or what made Earth? Who or what made the universe? What came first the chicken or the egg? God's like Santa, the Big Bang Theory's the Tooth Fairy. Does it really even matter? We're here! Smell the roses. And then die. Whatever."

New York City born and raised, she had bubble gum pink hair, a lip ring, an eyebrow ring, and a *lot* of tattoos. And she insisted on calling me "J". Oh yeah, and she hated life. She said that was why she was here, but I didn't get it. She'd tell me things, but not like Joe would.

"They can't deal with the fact that I hate life. It's not like I'm gonna commit suicide or anything, shit. Why can't I just give the finger to society and conformity and this entire fucked-up planet? Robbie Thompson!"

"Who's 'they'?" I thought maybe I was onto something, finally! Tara must know something that Joe didn't.

"I dunno, that's just what I call them." She smacked her lips.

"Call who?"

"*Them*. Whoever thought it was funny to pile us all in here like farm animals."

"So why'd you choose to be here if you hate it so much?"

"Choose? You think I chose to be here? Psh. I thought you and Joe talked. Judy Hajek!"

"He won't tell me anything about anyone else. He says he 'might as well give me your file'."

"Hmm. What a standup guy. Whatever. Woulda been nice for him to save me the breath. Look, I just showed up here one day, just like you."

"But you're alive…"

"Right."

"And you get paid to be here, this is your job?"

"Yup."

"And you didn't try to kill yourself?"

She took one of her iPod earpieces out and sighed. "I told you, no. I show up here, Ruth the Wretch tells me to 'pay attention', and that was that."

"What do you think you're supposed to be paying attention to?"

"Who the fuck knows, who the fuck cares." She put her earpiece back in.

"How long have you been here?" I asked, louder.

"'Bout half a year. Nina Garza!" My heart skipped a beat. I watched a teenager walk through the door. Why was I even excited? Garza wasn't even her maiden name. But just hearing her first name gave me a strange feeling of hope. I returned to my window, where she was fast asleep.

And then I watched the love of my life fall in love. His name was David, he was a physical therapist. They met at the grocery store. I don't really want to get into it. But he made her blush and I was jealous and happy and depressed as hell all at the same time. It had been long enough.

It had been five years in the waiting room. Can you imagine? Five years of one room, watching the world change, wearing the same damn suit.

Joe and I had long ago decided that I was the official "newcomers' counselor." Any people appearing to be confused and needing a little more guidance than the trusty old handbook—that's where I came in. I told them everything I knew. Besides the fact that I didn't work there…I didn't want to cause any more outbursts. I comforted them, joked that maybe I'd "see them next time," and then called their name and led them to their grand exit.

"Hey Joe, what would happen if I decided to walk through the door?"

"You'd just end up right back here."

"Of course." He'd explained that when he walks through the door every night, he's just magically sitting in his car, as if he just pulled up to his house.

"What do you tell people?" I'd asked.

"That I do programming. Most people don't know much about it and that's what I wanted to go to college for. They never ask questions."

Even more amazing, he told me that he's been dating a woman for three years.

"She works a night job too, so it works out. She manages a motel."

"Do you think you'll ever tell her the truth?"

"Oh, I can't. That's like, the one rule. I think my deal would be off the table if I told."

"What, you'd just die all the sudden?"

"I don't know! I'm not risking it."

"But you told me. Maybe that's why Ruth won't talk."

"I've told you, you're obviously an exception. You practically work here too. Ruth's just traditional. She probably thinks you're some sort of spy or demon or somethin'."

"Spy for who, the devil? C'mon Joe."

He roared a laugh and I could smell his microwaved pizza dinner. At least I didn't have to see bits of food caught in his braces anymore, he'd finally gotten them taken off. "I don't know Jude! You've barely been here! Let her warm up to our newest pain in the ass dead guy." Another roar.

But now it had been five years and still nothing out of Ruth. I spent my nights swapping stories with Joe and watching our wives (they got engaged my first year there) out of the window together. I considered it "meeting his family"...even though he was breaking the rules by showing me. Employees aren't allowed to "use the windows". But he wanted to show me everything—his Chicago apartment, his favorite bar, his dog.

"She sure is a looker," he'd said about Nina.

But mostly, I was meeting a ton of newly dead. It was fascinating and it kept my mind off waiting. I've met people who have died from just about every way there is to die. Tornadoes, hurricanes, earthquakes, tsunamis, heart attacks, shipwrecks, plane wrecks, car wrecks, lightning, dog attacks, shark attacks, knives, bullets, strangling, burning, starvation, cancer, poisoning, strokes, falling, frost bite, snake bites, peacefully in your sleep...you name it, I've heard it. I met more people than I had even come close to meeting in my 30-year lifespan. I was a little bit of a social butterfly. I met cowboys and city slickers, homeless people and famous people, criminals and preachers, inventors, politicians, singers, actors, writers, people of all ages and races and backgrounds...I met a man who had spent his entire life making picture frames. He said none of his other lives had been as fulfilling.

"I created places to hold memories. What more can a man do?" He was all wrinkles and smiles. I didn't want his name to be called. There wasn't much happiness in the waiting room, ever.

Every once in a while, a basket would appear on a near-by seat. Joe would have to get up and check the name and then carry it through the door when it was time. Sometimes he would pray over the tiny, wiggling bodies. Sometimes they'd be wailing and the whole room would get deathly quiet. Some people would cry to themselves.

One night I asked Tara what happened with miscarriages. She was great for sensitive questions because, well, she wasn't sensitive. At all.

"They never come here unless they're actual *babies*. Like six months in the belly at least I'd say."

"So the others…don't get to live another life?"

"I dunno. Ask the Wretch. She's the only one that would know. They probably just don't want to make us deal with a disgusting bloody mess, ya know? They probably just go straight to their new lives."

"Yeah." This is definitely not heaven, I thought for the millionth time.

And that's why I got nervous when I watched the love of my life have children. But they were both healthy. They were so beautiful. Nina didn't name them what we'd talked about. I was glad. I didn't want to feel like they were mine. David was a good man and a good father. I lived through him. I tried not to watch when they had sex.

And then I watched them grow old together.

I did work up the nerve to ask Ruth about the babies one day. She glared at me for awhile and then said, "Of course they get another life. This is not a cold place, Mr. Floyd, no matter what you'd like to believe."

"It's just very mechanical. So systematic, so emotionless."

"That's the way it has to be. Just like on Earth, without regulation and government, there would be chaos."

"So what would you call my situation?"

"Merely a flaw in the system. You're not special, Mr. Floyd. Your love is not deeper than every other marriage in the world."

"Well, thank you for reminding me why I don't talk to you." I started to walk away.

"You'll be happy then, that the sub is coming in. I have to leave early today." I had wondered, in the beginning, how Ruth, Joe, and Tara could work literally every single day. After a few weeks, Joe left one night and a beautiful blonde woman replaced him.

"Have fun," Joe had whispered, patting me on the back before he stepped through the door.

"Hey, where's Tara?"

"Oh, you must be Jude. She's sick. I'm the sub, my name's Haley." She was gorgeous—tan, green eyes.

"Nice to meet you. I was wondering how they all can stand working so much."

"Well most of them need the money and really do enjoy work. The funny thing is, it's not like you can 'call in.' I guess God just knows if you're truly sick or if you have something really important to do. You'll think you're about to appear here, but you'll just stay in bed. And that's when I appear."

"That's crazy."

"Isn't everything? Tina Phan!"

"So you believe in God too?"

"Who else could pull something like this off?" She grinned and then grabbed my hand and pulled me around to her side of the desk. "Come here." It was nice to feel a woman's touch again—something other than the occasional handshake I get from newcomers.

She pulled out a thick binder and opened it. "Pick one." They were CDs!

"Wow. I didn't know we could…"

"Well Ruth doesn't allow it, Joe isn't really one for music, and Tara's kind of music is only suitable for her iPod." She pulled out a small stereo from under the desk. "Melvin Topp!"

I flipped through the binder. An Elvis Greatest Hits cover caught my eye. I laughed. "I haven't heard music in three weeks, but I haven't heard Elvis in years."

She grinned and put it in, turning the volume all the way up. It felt amazing to hear music blaring so close to my ear. Listening through the window isn't the same. Everything's kind of muted from the waiting room.

"Good to see you again Haley!" someone yelled from across the room.

Pretty soon at least half the room was dancing to "All Shook Up." Haley bounced around the room, greeting everyone, carrying her list with her, and convincing people to dance through the door instead of walk when it was their turn.

It was the most fun I'd had waiting. I looked forward to Tara's sick days and Ruth's once a year, weekend long vacation (she lived and breathed the waiting room). Sometimes I even wished Joe would have things to do more often. I felt guilty about it, but playing poker and having paper airplane races got real old, real fast.

Plus, Haley always brought me the best food. Ruth stuck to a sandwich and fruit since my very first day. Joe would usually bring pizza or burgers. Tara was unpredictable. Sometimes it was just candy, other times it was Ramen. But Haley cooked. Roast beef, honey-glazed salmon, Thai shrimp, chicken gumbo...delicious. I felt bad that they were bringing me food for awhile, but Joe told me that they'd all received a small raise.

"So, you really think you're waiting for your wife?" Haley asked me that day I met her.

"Yes."

"That's so sweet." Something about the way she said it, I knew she didn't believe it.

"You believe in God, but not in the fact that I'm waiting?"

"I'm sorry, it's just...God wouldn't do this. Trap you in here. And not give others the chance to do the same. It just doesn't make sense."

"Well I guess we'll never know, huh? Where are you from, anyway?"

"Tiny town in Iowa."

"And what's your story if you don't mind me asking?"

"You mean, how'd I get here?"

"Yeah."

"Well, I actually just needed a job." She blushed. "But I mean, that's not why I was hired. It's not like anyone can work here."

"What *are* the qualifications?"

"Well, for starters you have to be able to keep a secret. Plus, I guess we all have to bring something to the table. Or I guess you could say there has to be some end result in us having the job. Like, you know Joe's reason, similar to Tara's."

"Well, yeah, I get Joe's. But Tara..."

"Really? It's simple. She doesn't see beauty in anything. She appreciates nothing, she sees life as a forced step before death."

"And working here is going to change that?"

She gave me a bewildered look. "Of course. Every day, she sees people who made something out of their lives. And then she sees them walk through that door and start it all over again. She sees the possibility that we're all given. One day she'll get it. The minute Joe was given a second chance, he turned his life around. That was all it took to prove to him that he could have a purpose. It takes some people longer."

"And you?"

"Well, I was studying grief counseling. When my mom died, I saw a grief counselor and she literally saved me—I wanted to help others like she'd helped me. But when my dad died about a year ago, I quit school. He was all I had. How could I help people get through a loved one's death when I couldn't even get over one, you know?"

"So you've been here ever since?"

"Yup. I love it. Amie and Loren Mikeska!"

"Do the people whose names get called together end up together again in their new lives?" We both watched a smiling young couple walk through the door holding hands.

"That's what they think, and I don't ever disagree. But no. They've just been placed at the same time." And then she turned on "Hound Dog" and went to go dance with a young boy who'd been sulking in a chair.

Joe's honeymoon was a couple years into my "stay." A whole week of Haley. At the time, I wasn't aware that she was falling in love with me. But she did have a way of getting me away from the window.

"Jude!" She arrived in lipstick and dresses, hugs and homemade cakes.

"Hey stranger. Ready to work more than twice a month?"

"Oh, shut up. I do miss this place."

I scoffed. "You're crazy. All I want is to leave…" The week before that, I got tired of thinking about it and ran through the door, Ruth screaming at the top of her lungs the whole time. Joe was right. I just felt like I was falling through clouds for a second and then BAM! Slammed down right on my ass in the waiting room. These people had no sense of humor.

"Well I promise to make this week more exciting than ever." She sounded like I had hurt her feelings. I felt bad, but what did she expect? Her and Joe, and even

Tara—these people were my best friends now, but it wasn't real. I wasn't real.

"I don't think you can top your dance-offs." I mustered a smile.

"We'll see about that." She pulled out all the stops. One day she brought a projector and we watched movie after movie with popcorn and soda. We had hula hoop contests, three-legged races, egg and spoon races, and even eating contests. No wonder people thought this was heaven. A beautiful blonde woman handing out pie and cookies? Yeah, I would've believed it too.

The week flew by. She'd thought of everything. She even brought me new clothes (Joe's hand-me-downs were loose and stained, but they were better than wearing my suit all the time). We played video games like two kids, read magazines, and basically told each other our life stories. Of course, my story ended abruptly while she had a new story for every day. I figured she knew what she was to me; a distraction, an escape. We played Monopoly, Trouble, Clue, and every other board game you can think of. That's a long way from sensual if you ask me, unless you're playing Strip Scrabble, like me and Nina used to.

But at the end of that week, she kissed me. I let it happen for an instant and then jerked away.

"Haley, I'm married."

"No, you're dead."

"Reason Number Two."

"She's not waiting for you, Jude. She's with someone else, you've seen that for yourself."

"She's been on a couple dates, yes." I admit that at this point, I wasn't expecting Nina to marry the guy. "But she doesn't have to wait for me. She doesn't know about this place. The point is, *I'm* waiting for *her*. I'm sorry." Her eyes watered and then she noticed that some people were watching us. She stood up and brushed a tear away, heading to her desk.

"Tommy Norris!" Her voice cracked. I walked up to the desk.

"Haley…"

"It's fine, don't worry about it. I just thought…it's been so long."

"I know. And we've had so much fun together. You've kept me sane."

"Yeah. I guess I just mistook that for something else." She smiled, but her lip was still barely quivering. I felt like an asshole. Had I been leading her on this whole time?

"I'm so sorry, Haley. You're beautiful. And some guy who's actually alive is gonna be so lucky to have you. You deserve someone who can do more than play Parcheesi with you at your job." She grinned, unwillingly. "You understand, right?"

"How do you know you're waiting for her, though? How do you know you're not here so that you can meet me?"

I hesitated. I didn't want to tell her that she was just a 24-year-old with a crush and that Nina was my soul mate. So I settled on the cliché and cryptic, "I just know."

I spent 52 years in the waiting room, never aging, just watching and waiting.

I was "reunited" with Jake, the surfer, twice.

"I live dangerously, what can I say dude." It was cliff diving that first time I'd met him, climbing Everest the second time, and lastly, hang gliding. "In all my lives, I've never lived a day over 50. More bang for your buck, am I right?" he flashed his dimples.

I just laughed. "I gotta say, Jake, I've been in this room for over 50 years and yet I still don't envy you one bit."

"Man, don't be a hater."

I watched Nina retire and travel and play with her five grandchildren.

Most of the years seemed to drift by, but some days were harder than watching my funeral. Like watching my parents' funerals. Watching Nina's parents' funerals. Watching my brother's funeral. The day Tara announced she wouldn't be returning. After 10 years, she was still her strange self. And she was still a skeptic and a pessimist. But she got the message. She was ready to start living her life instead of resenting it. She was almost 30 now, but she was still a little sister to me.

"I'll miss ya' J." I had never seen her cry. I had hardly ever even seen her smile with teeth. Now I got to see both. She turned off her iPod and everything.

"I'll be watching you." I pointed to the windows and made a creepy face. "And I'll miss you too." I walked her to the door with my arm around her shoulder.

"Do me a favor, J?"

"Anything for you, dear."

"When she gets here, tell her that you helped me get my life on track."

"Oh, c'mon Tara, you did that all by yourself."

She smiled. "No. It was you and her. Your crazy story. Your waiting."

I waved her words away. "Just take care of yourself. And keep studying for that chem test; you know it's gonna be harder than you think. And tell your boyfriend that if he—"

"Jude. I got it."

"Ok, ok." I squeezed her hand. "Adios."

She squeezed back. "After awhile, crocodile."

And then, "Please step away from the doorway, Mr. Floyd." Ruth's shift had begun. I can say that in ten years, she *had* become more friendly…but you had to really pay attention. She had started mixing up the whole sandwich routine and one day she had even said, "Can you watch things out here for a bit? I have to step in the back." It was progress.

"Ruth, Ruth, Ruth. So good to see you today. Is that a new hairstyle?"

"I'm an old woman, Jude. What do you want today?" She had her hand on her hip, as usual. I figured if I kept asking questions, one day she'd answer. That hadn't really proved true yet.

"Hey, you called me Jude." She slipped sometimes.

"Don't push your luck."

"I just wanted to know what was going to happen now that Tara's gone. How do you find a replacement?"

"Joan Anderson!" She sighed deeply. "I have a stack of

resumes to go through. No different than any other job."

"But how is that possible? You're not looking for education or experience...this isn't 'just like any other job'."

"I decide who needs this the most."

"So you didn't need this? You're just a decision maker who works for them? Or are you one of them?"

"Mr. Floyd, I must say, you're making absolutely no sense."

"*Them*. That's what Tara called it."

"Called *what* exactly?

"Whatever or whoever is running this place!"

Ruth chuckled slowly. "All these years, and you still can't fathom the idea that The Waiting Room could be simply a phenomenon? An existence? A happening? Why do you not question life? Who's orchestrating that?"

"That's different. There's evolution and adaptation and recorded history and technology. There's a logical explanation for everything except this place."

"Parker Samson! And how do you know there's not?"

"Well, no one's told me if there is!"

"Do you know how many thousands of years it took for Darwin to come around? Perhaps The Waiting Room is just waiting to be discovered." The corners of her mouth twitched.

"You're fucking with me. And I don't appreciate it." I walked over to the window, where Nina was getting her kids ready for school and David was making pancakes. Cocky bastard.

"Jude." The old wretch had followed me. "I've been here since the beginning and I still don't have the answers. I promise."

"I don't even get that, Ruth."

"Since my first life, this has been my job. That was a very, very, very long time ago. I was the first manager."

"But how do you remember your lives? I thought you could only do that when you died."

"Correct."

"So you're dead?"

"No. Unfortunately, I'm still in my first life. I'm not sure when or if I'll ever die. But I think I'll stop aging soon. It took me more than a thousand years to look this old." She looked sincere, but my eyes were wide with disbelief.

"So how old *are* you then?" Ruth, immortal? This had to be one of Joe's pranks.

"I stopped counting long ago." But how would he get Ruth in on the prank…

"But why is that unfortunate? Isn't it kind of great, always getting to be the real you?"

She shook her head. "Think about how many people I've cared about—all gone forever." She looked away. This was not a prank. "So eventually, you stop getting attached to anyone… or anywhere. I've lived in ten different countries so far. I know the language of each."

"*Ten?*" I was impressed.

"It's nice not having to drive to work." She smiled. "And you'd think it'd be nice not having anything holding you down. I've travelled the world, but most of it alone."

I didn't know how to respond, so I went with another question. "So you really have no idea who pays you every week?"

"I only have guesses. But I highly doubt it's a 'who'. Saoirse Nabokov!" She pronounced every name perfectly—every nationality, every accent mark and tilde. Not like the others (especially Joe). "I've had a lot of practice," she said after catching me sounding out the girl's name silently.

"So what then, if not a 'who'?"

"Just a system. Put in place for a reason. I guess you all have to have somewhere to go while the universe figures out where to put you."

"But what happened before you came along? I mean, this place was still here, right?"

"Yes. Someone left me one sheet of explanation. But they had no idea what they were doing. Back then, there was only one employee. All by themselves, probably not doing a very good job. My guess? It was overwhelming, having a secret about humanity and not being able to share it with anyone. I got here and resumes for my 'helpers' started piling up."

"So what happened to that person?"

"Well, he or she either wasn't made to live as long as I have or they messed up."

"Messed up?"

"Told someone. Went mad. Wouldn't you?"

I stared at her for a second. "I don't think you've ever talked to me for this long. And it's been a decade."

She laughed. One of the first times I had heard that sound. "You were a curveball. It's my job to keep things running smoothly around here you know. You made that hard."

"But now you know I'm here to stay?"

"I'm starting to accept that."

"Do you still think I'm 'merely a flaw in the system'?"

"It's possible. Honestly, I think we're all waiting."

"For what?"

"For her time. That's when we'll know I guess. Ana Cantu!"

So we all waited. But not all of us made it. Another decade passed and Joe didn't come in for his shift one night. I knew he hadn't planned anything, so I figured he was sick. I took my focus off of Nina and concentrated on the thought of Joe and his wife and his kids and Chicago. The windows were intelligent. I had started calling them computers. You couldn't just spy on anyone. You had to really know the person, know enough to gain entrance into a personal viewing of their life.

Joe wasn't sick. He'd had a heart attack at the age of 61. You're not supposed to feel like this after you die. You're supposed to be happy and free and, you know, all that garbage people tell you when someone dies. "Don't worry, they're in a better place now." Yeah fucking right.

I couldn't believe he was gone. I leaned against the glass and cried. I'd never had a better friend or a longer friendship.

I thought about the time he'd offered to go visit Nina. This was in the first few months. He saw how uneasy I was, watching her.

41

"You know…I could go see her." He'd almost whispered.

"What are you talking about?"

"Nina. If you want."

"You're allowed to do that?"

"Well, I mean, it's not in the rules or anything…since, ya' know, nobody's ever stayed here long enough to even tell us a whole lot about their lives."

"She's in Texas."

"I know. I could drive. Or call." That's when I knew what kind of man he was. I'm ashamed to say I thought about his offer for a long time. But then I realized.

"Joe, you'd lose your job. Even if you did visit her, you can't tell her about this place. That *is* in the rules."

"Yeah, but I could tell her, I dunno, that you're safe or happy or somethin'. I'm just sayin', I'd do it if you wanted me to."

I clapped him on the back. "Knowing Nina, she'd think you were a psycho and try to kick your ass. But thanks for the offer buddy. Seriously. But do you know how much worse this all would be if you got kicked out of the little club?" I shuddered.

Joe was…Joe. He was the best.

"Why hasn't he come here yet?" I asked Haley, who had obviously shown up. I thought she'd replace Tara, but she didn't want the graveyard shift.

Instead, it was Harry, an elderly man who was almost blind and deaf. "I can't sleep during those goddamn hours anyway," he'd said.

Turns out, Ruth hired him because he thought he could outrun death. I'm not even kidding. This 80-something year old man had decided to waste his entire savings, leaving nothing for his family, on freezing and preserving his body. He thought he'd wake up after awhile and just… keep on living. Ruth said, "That kind of talk is just bull and people need to know it." He worked in the waiting room for about three years, finally got the point (more from Ruth's incessant ranting than the actual work), went home and revised his will, and died the next day.

But anyway, now Haley was taking over Joe's shifts and Ruth would find another sub.

"Same reason your parents or your brother never came here I guess. There are a lot of waiting rooms, Jude."

I was always scared that she was only trying to get closer to me. The way she looked at me sometimes. I didn't like the idea of her being there every night. But she never tried to kiss me again. Sometimes I wished she would. Even though now, she was now over ten years older than me, physically I mean. But she was still beautiful. A little gray was peeking through her blonde, blonde hair. You'd think I would've given up my "waiting" by now. I mean, after all, it's in a man's nature; it's a legitimate physical need. And it's not like Nina wasn't getting any. But to be honest, it wasn't hard. First of all, having sex in the waiting room would've felt like having sex in a church or the ER. Secondly, I cared about Haley too much to let her fall even more in love with someone she could never have. And lastly, I didn't know the repercussions! This might sound stupid, but I thought that if I didn't "properly" wait for Nina, I wouldn't be allowed to wait anymore. I thought my name would just pop up on the list. It's a valid point.

What's the use in loyally waiting if you're not going to be loyal?

"So there's zero amount of determining fate for which room you go to?"

"Not unless you die together. Those people usually aren't split up. It's just like our lists. You'd think that having the lists means our deaths are predetermined, but the names don't show up in the system *until* the person has died. There is no such thing as fate." She looked down. I had never really heard her so…realistic. I thought about when I first met her, the optimistic, bubbly, naïve girl. "You do always come back to the same room though. You know that. Not that it matters. The only thing that stays the same in these places is the manager."

She still played music and baked, she still loved her job, but she wasn't really happy. She was still alone. But she still brought me things to devour: food, books, crossword puzzles. I guess you're never too old or too dead to read *The Catcher in the Rye* for the first time (I literally did nothing in high school).

So Joe's poker games were over, as was our fantasy football. No more pizza or burgers. No more snuck-in cigars or whiskey. It was never the same after that.

Harry's replacement was Quinton, a gay teenager who'd jumped off a bridge. Well, he's not a teenager anymore, but when he started he was. The first time I met him, he said, "Everyone thinks suicide is so depressing. Wait till I tell them I was just applying for a job." I laughed my ass off.

But other than the occasional hilarious joke, Quinton

was extremely quiet. He was an artist, and spent his entire shift drawing, getting caught up and calling names late.

I felt like the grim reaper. Watching everyone around me age and leave, age and die, marry and have kids, get their PhD (Haley)…

"How the hell do you do it?" I broke down and asked Ruth one day.

"Do what?" she asked innocently.

"Just…watch. Never participate, never die—never even get sick!"

"You miss allergies?" She raised an eyebrow.

"You get the point, Ruth. I'm going nuts." I slumped down in the nearest chair.

"Alexandra Woodmansee! What can I tell you? You'll never get used to it. That's just that. Besides, isn't it everyone's dream to look 30 forever?"

"Ha-ha. At least I'll always have you…yay."

"Your sarcasm really hurts," she said, sarcastically of course. I blinked at her.

"Nina used to say that."

She sighed. "I'm here if you need to talk." She started walking away.

I punched the back of the chair. Ruth flinched. "You don't get it! This is your job or punishment or redemption, whatever it is to you! BUT IT'S DIFFERENT FOR ME! I'M TIRED OF WAITING! I DON'T WANT TO DO IT ANYMORE!"

Immediately after I said it, I regretted it. I thought of the waiting room as some kind of force. I felt like I was being watched constantly and if I did the wrong thing or said the wrong thing—that was it, no second chances, no waiting. In my mind, I pictured me and Nina starting another life together as…the same people, with the same faces and memories. I thought that if we were special enough to wait for each other, then we must be special enough to live together, as ourselves, forever. I wasn't about to mess that up, even though I knew it was next to impossible.

But anger was expected. I definitely had my fair share of meltdowns over the 52 long years. I probably punched every single chair and window in that room. I even tried to start a fight with some guy because he "gave me a look." I was bored.

My most common breakdowns consisted of watching Nina and pretending that I was there next to her, having a complete conversation with her, cooking with her, kissing her, laughing with our children. I'd just press myself against the glass and stare into her life and get lost in it. People thought I was insane, babbling to myself. It usually didn't take me long to snap out of it and realize what a pathetic mess I was. David would get home from work or something and ruin my imaginary game.

Sometimes, I would lie. I told some people they were in Heaven and that after they walked through the door, they'd receive their first wings. I told others they were in Hell and I was Satan.

"I'm really not such a bad guy," I'd say. "People make me out to have a pitchfork and little horns…I don't know where they get these ideas. Do you see any fire?"

Of course, this was only fun with newbies who hadn't received packets yet. I learned this quickly, when I told a man who had just finished with his seventh life that we'd all been abducted and we'd soon be probed. That was the first time I'd ever been punched, and yes, you can apparently bleed after you die.

I even convinced one woman that I was Jesus with a haircut. And one kid definitely believed that we were "The Chosen Ones" handpicked to save the universe from Evil.

Quinton told me that I better hope none of those people died again before I was gone. He had a good point, but that sure would make for an interesting day.

I thought about what Ruth had said, about me and Nina's love not being any different than anyone else's. I thought about all of our fights—the ones over how to order fast food and the ones about getting married in the first place...Ruth was probably right. We were probably just a glitch, and I was fine with that. But then other times, I thought about how we'd met and how fast we fell madly, crazy in love. And I thought, yeah, I can see how we'd be the only ones in the entire world that get to wait for each other.

I mean, don't get me wrong, it wasn't some fairy tale, chick flick meeting. But it was still cute as hell. I delivered a pizza to her dorm room freshman year. Yes, I was a pizza delivery boy. And yes, it was probably the best job I ever had. I drove around campus and listened to music all night, got as much free pizza as I wanted, and I was tipped with cases of beer or a phone number on more than one occasion. What more can an 18-year-old boy ask for?

Nina, however, was not one of those phone-number-tipping girls. The whole idea is kind of stupid anyway, because if you order a pizza, the delivery guy already has your number. I guess it's more of a gesture. But she did steal my pen. Now this may come as a shock to you, but most freshman boys don't carry around "spare pens." Therefore, she stole my only pen, which I needed for the next delivery. So I just went back to her dorm room. No other idea occurred to me.

"Uh...yeah?" She was chewing a large bite of cheese and mushroom.

"Yeah, hi. I think you kept my pen."

"Oh. Um..." She looked around. "No, I don't think I did."

"Well I had it when I delivered to you and now I don't. And I don't have another one so..." She was cute, but I had other deliveries to make. I was not going to let this little girl with glasses and flowery pajama pants slow me down.

"Okaaaaay, well here." She grabbed a pen from her desk (she had a coffee mug filled with them). She looked annoyed.

"Wow. Are you sure?"

"Uh...it's just a pen. Yeah. It's all good." I followed her eyes to her TV screen.

"Are you really watching *The Sound of Music*?" It was a Saturday night.

"Yes. It's like, the best movie ever." She got very defensive.

"Calm down, I've never even seen it. I'm just sayin'..." She thought I was a complete idiot. It probably didn't help that I was staring at her boobs.

"You've never seen *The Sound of Music*? You're joking right?" Her pretty eyes got real wide.

"C'mon, it's not like it's *The Matrix* or somethin'. Wow, are all those books for school?" I stared in awe at her bookshelf.

"Uh, no."

"You read those for fun?" She was such a nerd.

"Yup." She started closing the door slowly. "And what do you do, play computer games all night?" I wasn't hard to peg, apparently.

"Well, technology is the future. Books will die out eventually." I knew I was going to rock the boat with that one.

I stood in the hallway for an hour—arguing with her, flirting with her, and eventually making plans to have a movie marathon the next night (she'd never seen *The Matrix*, what the hell!). The deliveries in my car were cold and I almost got fired. Almost. And that was it. We became inseparable. And I never found that damn pen. But I'm glad it was lost.

CHAPTER 3

So 52 years. Sounds crazy, right? You'd think I would've gone mad. But I was too preoccupied watching the entire world change. It's much more shocking when you're just watching the change instead of experiencing it. I thought of Ruth experiencing all the different centuries. I wondered which one she liked best...

And then one day, I didn't have to wait anymore. I watched in horror as the wrinkled grandmother that used to be my wife died in a hospital bed, holding her daughter's hand. I wanted her to keep on living; I knew she had a few good years left in her. But at the same time, I was literally giddy. And I hated myself for it. But I knew she'd appear before my eyes in seconds. I was so nervous. I paced back and forth, my eyes darting around the room. Ruth tapped her nails on the desk loudly.

And there she was. She materialized next to me just like so many others had done. At first, she was the same woman that had died—wispy white hair and faded brown eyes. But then she saw me and her face lit up. She changed into my Nina, 30-year-old stunning Nina.

"J-Jude?" She looked down at her perfectly smooth hands and then touched my face.

"I'm here. I'm real." We cried and hugged and kissed for what seemed like hours.

"So this is Heaven?" she asked, her face was pink and wet with tears.

"No, baby, this isn't Heaven." Her face scrunched in confusion. I hadn't even noticed that Ruth had walked up to us.

"Hi, I'm Ruth." Nina stuck out her hand instinctively and then Ruth just hugged her, beaming. I chuckled.

"Jude?" I remembered how I felt my first day.

"Well, Ruth? Are you gonna give her a packet or can I do the honors?"

"I'll be at my desk." She shook her head and I could've sworn I saw her wipe away a tear.

"Wait, Ruth? Have...have our names showed up yet?" I was so scared, suddenly very aware of time.

"No. I have a feeling you two will have longer than most," she said with a smile.

I sat Nina down, smoothed her hair, traced her lips, and told her everything.

Of course, her first response was, "So you've been watching me this whole time?" Women. They can never look at the big picture. It's always the fine print.

Her next contribution to the conversation was not what I expected. "Well, it must be God." Neither one of us had been religious in our life together. We lived like any Agnostics in Christian families—discreetly. But now she was here, with me, her husband who had died 52 years ago, so she was taking the Joe-Haley approach. "It's too insane to be anything else. I guess we were wrong."

I just stared at her. "For now, can we just agree to disagree? I have no idea how much time we have." By then, it had been over two hours. Ruth had been switching her gaze from us to the list, us to the list. People that were showing up just assumed we'd died together.

I couldn't decide whether or not to waste time telling her about everything that I'd experienced and everyone I'd met—or if I should just shut up and not take my hands or lips off of her. I settled with a mix of both.

"I feel so guilty." Her bottom lip quivered.

"Why baby?"

"You've just been here waiting for me and watching me and I was just off getting remarried and-"

"Nina, stop. You did exactly what I wanted you to do. I wanted you to be happy, with or without me. The world wouldn't have been the same without you."

"But *my* world wasn't the same without *you*."

We cried into each other's necks and then laughed when we saw each other's blotchy, swollen faces. I felt closer to her than I ever had before. And then I felt sad that this, this small moment in time after my wife died and before we had to start all over, this was quite possibly the happiest I had ever been.

"I'm so glad you stole my pen that night." She giggled and snuggled closer in my arms.

"I did not steal your pen, for the last time. But I'm glad you *thought* I did." She smiled so big with her fake dimples.

Ruth decided to stay past her shift, letting Haley know

not to come in. I was glad. Not only because I thought it'd be awkward, but I wanted Ruth there. She knew the most, she'd been there the longest, and if anyone was going to know what the hell was happening to us—it'd be Ruth.

"You don't think we're waiting on someone else, do you?" Nina asked after a few more hours.

"Like who?"

"Well I don't know…" I caught her sneaking glances out the window. Of course. She had a family. I felt selfish. She'd probably been dying to stare out the window this whole time.

"David. Your kids. Of course. I just…I don't think I'd still be here, waiting with you, you know?" I tried to say it as delicately as possible.

"Yeah, I know. It's just been so long. Everyone else's names are called so soon."

"I'm sure they're just trying to find the perfect place for us. We deserve it."

"It just sounds so stupid when you say 'they'. Like, what do you think? That there's some secret, invisible oligarchy up here, playing eenie meeny miney moe on a map and then sending people there?"

"That's basically what people say God does. You know this. I just think it is what it is. The existence of this place doesn't prove there's a God just like the existence of Earth doesn't prove there's a God."

"Jude, it's not the same. This place is…special."

I looked around. "Have you seen this place? It's an airport terminal. The only thing special about it is that you're in it."

She just shook her head. That's when I asked Ruth if we could step into the break room for a bit. Suddenly the whole place didn't feel so much like a church or an ER...I gave Ruth a significant look and was extremely surprised when she answered with a simple "Sure."

I made love to my wife 52 years after I died, four hours after she died, on an Employees Only table in some sort of afterlife holding pen. If that's not amazing, I don't know what is.

"See?" I asked, breathless and sticky. "You really think God would've let that happen?"

"If there is a God, he's not a prude."

She pulled me onto the floor.

Ruth was knocking, but it took us awhile to wake up and realize what was happening. She finally just barged in with her hands covering her eyes.

"I'm trying to be nice here, Jude, but it's been three hours! I have to pee, I'm hungry, I'm thirsty, and I'm an old woman. I'm sorry, I can't hold it any longer!"

We busted out laughing and I was grateful that we put our clothes back on before we fell asleep. Emotional roller coasters are exhausting.

"We're sorry, Ruth, we fell asleep. It's ok, you can uncover your eyes."

"Oh. Ok. I thought you were being a little too quiet." We were grinning sheepishly like two kids caught "necking" in a backseat. After all, yesterday, Nina was in her eighties and I had at least *felt* like I was the same age. Now we both felt 18 again.

"Sorry, Ruth. We'll go man the desk. Take your time."

I let Nina call out some names and I basked in my new-found happiness. I was secretly hoping that our names would never show up on the list.

"How can people be so nonchalant about going through the door?" She was fascinated with this. "I'd be hysterical if you weren't here. I'd refuse to go. I'd just watch my kids until someone carried me out."

"Some of these people have done this hundreds of times. It's nothing to them, just something that has to be done. Plus, they all know that not walking through the door could possibly leave you with no future—no new life to begin."

"Jelani Gowon! But is that really true?"

"Who knows. That's just what the packet threatens. It's depressing just watching though. You don't actually enjoy it like you'd think you would...Luckily, *I've* been here to explain that to new people, in case they're thinking what you're thinking. Most people don't want to chance it. Think about it, would you really risk not being able to live again, meet up with everyone you've ever cared about again?"

"But the packet says it's impossible to reconnect with anyone from your past." She'd skimmed through it earlier.

"Yeah, impossible to do it on purpose. But you never know. And then maybe you'd die at the same time, come to this room, and *know*."

"That's just too many ifs and maybes."

"But you still wouldn't risk it."

"You're right. But there have been people who still refuse, right? Even after they know the consequences?"

"Oh yeah. I've never seen it, but Ruth says if you don't go through the door within like 15 minutes of when your name was called, you just…disappear, as strangely as you get here, you leave the same way."

"Igor Smirnov! Wow. But she has no idea what really happens to them?"

"Nope. The door has to be there for a reason though. Tara used to say that it probably 'guided you,' like a slide out of a plane."

"That sounds fun."

"Yeah and Quinton says that you probably step through the door and land right into a womb or just start coming out of one."

"That's disgusting. No one's ever told you? It doesn't explain in the packet?"

"No one remembers, sweetie. Do you remember your birth? They say that they step through the door and the lights go off. And that's it. New life."

"And the packet?"

"Nothing. No details, as usual."

"Who wrote the packet?"

I laughed. "Ruth."

"What?!"

"Who were you expecting? Oh that's right, the man upstairs. Just like the Bible, huh?"

"So there was no explanation before her?"

"She said she was left brief instructions. She knew

that wouldn't be enough. So over the years, she gathered stories and wrote a handbook. It's vague because it's all she knows. Plus, she says she 'doesn't want to make assumptions'."

"You should tell her to add us."

"What do you mean?"

"Well this whole time, people thought it was impossible. To wait or to find someone again…Don't you think they should know that it is possible?"

"But we don't know that we'll find each other again."

"Do you really believe that? After you've waited this long?" She stroked my arms.

"Our names haven't even shown up yet. We could be here forever. Or maybe I wasn't waiting. Maybe we're both just 'glitches'." I had to think about all the options.

"You're the one that said 'they're' probably still placing us." She used finger quotes when she said "they're". Her voice was starting to sound irritated.

"I know, I know. I guess I just don't want to get my hopes up. And I don't want to say goodbye to you."

"Booger. Look at me." Her dark hair was messy and frizzy, her makeup was smeared, her clothes were wrinkled—and she was by far the most beautiful thing I'd ever seen. "We're going to live another life together, I know it, I can feel it. And this time, it won't be cut short. And if it is, guess what? I'll wait for you. Or you'll wait for me again. And then we'll start over, together. I promise."

I was staring at Ruth. She'd just walked back in and grabbed the latest sheet from the printer. Her face had turned whiter than the walls.

"How much longer, Ruth?"

She turned to look at me sadly. I realized that I had been one of the only consistent people in her life.

"A little over two hours."

I looked at Nina, who was tearing up.

"And our names showed up together?"

"Yes. Jude and Nina Floyd." Ruth looked shaky. She handed me the sheet.

"Well. I'm glad you have the right last name again."

"You *would* say that right now." Nina was crying and laughing and hugging her knees.

I took her hand. "So what do you want to do for our last two hours, my love?"

"Not our last."

"Well. Our last two hours…until next time?"

"Jude, our names were together. My name was changed back. That means something."

"You're right, you're right. I'm sorry for being so skeptical. I would just rather stay here with you."

"No, it's better this way. Think of all the things you never got to do, the places you've never been. We could wake up in Tuscany in 1920. We could own a vineyard. You could be the next president."

Ruth and I both laughed at that one.

Nina just smiled. "You never know," she said.

I put a hand on her stomach. "I just want to have babies and get old and fat and wrinkly with you."

"That sounds amazing. Maybe we can go through with that whole hot air balloon suicide thing this time."

Ruth was calling out names and trying to compose

herself, smoothing out her skirt compulsively. She looked over at me and winked. "Why don't you two go have some more privacy? You're drawing attention."

"You read my mind, Ruthie."

We talked about every possibility: where we'd end up, what time period, if we'd look anything like ourselves, if we'd have similar families, friends, jobs…if there was any way to remind ourselves of our first life together…

I wrote a goodbye note to everyone. After all, when I got back, only Ruth would be here probably. Maybe not even her. I was sure that one day, she'd get her chance to live a second life. So I tried writing a second goodbye note to Ruth, just in case. But it was too hard. So I settled with an "until next time" note. Surely she wouldn't be gone by my next visit.

And then me and Nina decided to write notes to each other, in case one of us had to wait for the other…

"We only have an hour left." I kissed her long and hard, soaking up every touch and sound and scent.

She got up from her chair at the break room table and straddled me.

"I feel like we're dying. Saying goodbye forever. Like some horrible end-of-the-world movie."

I squeezed her thighs. "Well you know what the main characters always do when they think they're gonna die, right?"

"How did I know that was coming?" she laughed and wrapped her arms around me. I picked her up and thought, maybe Ruth is wrong. Maybe this is Heaven.

Before we knew it, Ruth was knocking again. I was re-minded of the time she tapped me awake with her long fake nails.

"Is it time already?" I asked her when she walked in (yes, we were dressed). I started to panic.

"You have about 15 minutes." Her eyes looked swollen. I got up and gave her a big hug. It dawned on me that I'd known her for 52 years and yet there was still so much I didn't know about her. I guess it's hard to learn about someone's life when they've been living it for hundreds of years.

"Here Ruthie, I wrote you a note. And here's a note for everybody else. And here's a note from me to Nina if she dies before me. And here's a note from her to me if...well, vice versa. Think you can handle it?"

"Yeah, sure kid."

"That sounds so much better than Mr. Floyd."

"Shut up." She grabbed the letters, which were neatly labeled, and stuck them in a drawer, sliding hers into her pocket.

"Do you think you'll be able to handle this place while I'm gone?" I winked. And then I felt like the infamous Jake Reynolds. He should be coming back soon...

"Hardly. You were the best unpaid employee I've ever had." We laughed and hugged again. I hadn't noticed that Nina was back in front of a window. I walked over to her.

"Missing them?"

"Yes. It sounds strange, but I feel like I was their mother a lifetime ago. They all just seem like a memory. A great one though."

I didn't know what to say. "Well don't worry, it never felt that way waiting for you. Maybe because I knew I was waiting. I mean, it felt like forever since I had kissed you…but at the same time, the feeling, the memory—it never faded."

She smiled up at me with tired eyes. "I hope we always get to wait together this long. Can you imagine only having a few minutes? To reminisce?"

"To do other things…"

"Yeah, yeah. You think it'll always be like this?"

"Probably. We have to go somewhere in time, into two lives that will one day cross, and still be virtually the same people…finding that exact place isn't an easy job I'm sure. But we can worry about that when the time comes."

I put my arm around her and we walked back to the desk.

"Five minutes," Ruth said. "I'm sorry, I'm not trying to be some sort of morbid countdown. I just thought you'd want to know."

"It's ok, we do." Nina took Ruth's hand and squeezed it. "I feel pressured though. What to do in your last five minutes of life or death or purgatory or whatever you want to call this?"

"If we were out in the world, I'd rush us out to go have ice cream. Or go lay in the park. Or go skinny dipping. Something great. But we're here." How disappointing. I racked my brain for something to do or say.

Nina shrugged her shoulders and look forlornly at the exit door.

"I have an idea." Ruth reached under the desk and pulled out a dusty CD player.

"Oh wow, I haven't seen one of those things in at least 40 years." Nina reached out and drew a line in the dust as she smoothed her finger over the radio buttons.

"It's Haley's. She hasn't played anything in a while..." Haley was in her 70s now. She had finally fallen in love—at the ripe age of 61. But sadly, he'd died only a few years after their wedding. She hadn't danced around the room since.

"Well, do you two have a song?" Ruth flipped through the old CD book.

"You've never allowed music." I eyed her.

"This is a special occasion."

Nina pointed to a CD. "That one. That was our song."

To be honest, we'd probably had about ten songs. Nina loved every kind of music so she pretty much picked a song from every genre and called it "our song." Whenever John Michael Montgomery's "I Love the Way You Love Me" came on, she'd put her hand on her heart and sing and kiss me and say, "I love this song. This should be our song." So I wondered which song she'd picked today.

Jason Mraz started playing loudly. "I'm Yours." People turned around, smiling. A 50-plus year old song was playing out of a 50-plus year old device. But I guess there's not really an "age" for things like that in the waiting room.

I remembered dancing to that song at our best friends' wedding. I was a groomsman and Nina was a bridesmaid.

I guess that was the first time we walked down the aisle together. The whole time I was thinking, man our wedding's gonna be so much cooler than this. And Nina was thinking, when *is* he gonna propose?

"You can dance out the door whenever. It's time." I kissed her on the cheek and Nina hugged her. "Goodbye you two. Have fun."

And then we danced.

Nina sang to me and swung her hips, her hands clasped around my neck.

I breathed in her hair and her faint, worn-off perfume. "I love you like frogs love flies."

"I love that book." She sighed and laid her head on my chest.

"You don't love me back?"

"I love you like pigs love pies."

We smiled and kissed and cried, dancing closer to the door.

"I'll be seeing you." It's true that all the best lines are taken.

"I love that song. That should be our song."

I grinned. "I was actually quoting The Notebook."

"I love that movie."

"I know." I noticed Ruth out of the corner of my eye. She was pointing to her watch. "How about: I'll wait for you. Every single time. Forever."

"I'll wait for you too." Her eyes spilled over as I kissed her all over her face. I tasted the familiar saltiness.

We danced into a bright light, shaking with sorrow, fear, and excitement.

Ruth reached in her pocket and unfolded the sheet of paper. Screw waiting.

Dear Ruth,

It's been some ride, huh? I'm going to miss you like crazy. You were like some sort of superhero, grandmother, mom, sister, and best friend all rolled into one.

We've been thinking… maybe you should add our story to the handbook? I know you won't want to and I know that it'll cause a lot of confusion and hope and questions. But maybe it's needed. Just promise me you'll think about it.

I'll miss you more than you know,
Jude

She wiped away a tear, folded the letter, and stuck it back in her pocket. And then she rolled her eyes. Add their story? Yeah right! Jude had no idea how difficult that would make things around here. As if it wasn't crazy enough to begin with. No way Jose was that about to happen.

It took all she had not to read their notes to each other. After a few years, she forgot they were even there.

Leah & Luke

She owned my favorite bakery in town, she never tried to

help me out the door, and I could hear her dimples in her voice, feel them throughout the whole room, taste them in her cupcakes. It was easy to fall in love with Leah. The first time I hugged her, I told her that her arm was covered in vowels.

"What?" She pulled away in confusion.

"A, E, O, I." I traced over the moles with my thumb.

"Oh, Braille."

"Yes."

That was at the end of our first date, and I didn't think I'd ever be able to walk into her shop again. But the next day, she showed up with chocolate cheesecake.

"The Sprinkles On Top chick is here!" I heard from my room.

It wasn't exactly a selling point that I lived with my sister, Aileen, especially since no one really liked her, but if anyone could make the best out of a situation, it was Leah.

"Sorry about her," I said once we were in the safety of my room. I was suddenly embarrassed. How terribly plain my room must look to her: a woman who creates worlds with icing.

"She'll warm up." That's all she said, just like that, already giving "us" more hope than I was. But even back then, she was talking about New York, and even back then, I knew she'd never stay.

I thought at any moment she'd realize how much better she could do.

"You can do better," Aileen had muttered after our third official date. My darling sister was protective in her own special way. She reeked of floss and sterilizing fluid, spent all her time at the clinic, and pined after her married, scrubs-clad boss.

"Don't be a bitch, she's practically a saint."

"You're not some charity family of six who needs her to pray for you and bring you meals."

"It's dessert, and that's what she loves."

"You're pathetic. Her dad is a minister." Aileen didn't trust religion. She didn't trust anyone or anything really, just me. She was basically my only family. Mom and Dad moved to a Florida retirement condo a long time ago. They had us when they were in their forties and I don't really think they were pleased with the results of their midlife crises.

So I told my sister that she was just jealous, in true stick-out-your-tongue fashion and that was basically the last time we talked about that. I think she finally conceded when introduced to Leah's banana nut bread-banana pudding combo. No one can resist that concoction, not even Satan.

But after our first kiss, I still didn't understand what I had to offer. Aileen was right. I'm a 39-year-old man working at a "research institute." And yes, that's a fancy way of saying, "call center." And yes, that's a fancy way of saying, "I persuaded people to take surveys and I wasn't even good at it." *She*, however, was a pastry chef. She went to the best culinary school in Alabama. I liked calling her a baker.

I wasn't even one of those musical genius blind men. My mother put me in piano, guitar, and cello lessons and I failed in all three. I sang even worse. People like Ray Charles really screwed up the world's expectations of us.

Oh, and no, I could not paint or sketch, or create anything magnificent from behind dark sunglasses. Two people in my life have told me I'm attractive: my mother and my high school girlfriend (who left me for the editor of the yearbook, Todd Spence). I could feel my thin hair receding. Aileen said it's okay, that hers was too.

But Leah found something I guess. Before I knew it, my new cologne was her spit. It had suddenly been a whole year, and all I wanted to do was float on my back in the waves of her hair, dive in and never come up, drown in the ruffles constantly attached to my fingers. The strands tickled my nose with the scent of flour. All I could think about was rigging the universe to give us ten more minutes kissing in the bakery pantry after hours. Our lips were probably tired of each other. She always fell asleep first, arm over belly button, nose against neck.

One day she said, "Our skin shades are like a Picasso painting." I didn't know what that really meant, but somehow, I appreciated it. I liked thinking of us lying next to each other on an artist's palette.

It was the love I'd always read about in books but never believed in.

The day I *really* knew though, was a "bland epiphany," as she puts it. She wanted the moment to be funny, maybe, or romantic. But it was just a candle.

We were sitting in the living room, tuning out the sound of Aileen singing Shakira (very badly) in the shower. I smelled the familiar scent of my sister's favorite candle.

"She's literally obsessed with that damn thing. She's burned it so much, I'm sure it's a centimeter high."

"Still quite tall actually."

Then she grabbed my hand. Her fingers felt like the taste of strawberry milk. She led me over to the small table outside Aileen's door and carefully wrapped my palms around the warm wax.

"See? It's pretty massive."

I had never cared about the damn candle, but suddenly, I cared about everything so much more than I ever had.

"What does it look like?"

She didn't even hesitate.

"It kind of looks like you and me."

"What?"

"The base is warm and rich like carrot cake or cinnamon coffee, fading towards the top like honey oatmeal cookies. And the tip is murky and soft, like coconut, like your eyes."

She said it so nonchalantly; it was just the way she spoke. But I soaked in every word out of her lips that smelled just like her bakery. I understood the color of a candle.

Leah was born with a gift of descriptions and I was born to hear them. All the while practicing my letters like in kindergarten, except on the body of a woman I loved rather than thick, bumpy papers.

She always talked about opening a fancy bakery in New York City and joked that I'd play violin in the subway for extra cash.

"We'll hold hands in Central Park and we'll call everyone Yankees. Save up for Rome, for London, for Paris."

She squeezed my elbows when she talked about all of this. Her palms were clammy like Pam on a cookie tray.

"You'd miss this magnificent house that has an actual porch and mailbox." She used to say she hated her apartment, that living in a room stacked on top of twenty other rooms is lonely.

"I'll make gourmet strawberry shortcake and tiramisu and we'll eat it with cheap wine and expensive music in a tiny apartment in Greenwich."

"And being able to drive! You love driving." I stroked the fine hairs on her stomach. And that's all I wanted to do, forever.

That day she picked me up from work was normal in every way. I was waiting outside with Aaron, who had just received his "one year cube of choice." Big day. Of course, he chose the cube next to mine. My cube of choice came years ago, and I sat on the end of the row, farthest away from our supervisor and closest to the bathroom. Aaron told me he was hanging up a picture of J-Lo, a Star Wars poster, and a Corvette calendar. Mine was bare, except a photo Leah had given me of us. No one had ever given me one. Everyone made a big deal out of that. "She has really pretty hair," Aaron had said. I thought that was weird since he usually talked about women in terms of ass and breast fistfuls.

Then he ranted about some old man that would only complete the survey if he could tell his life story at the same time.

"He was just going off, man. 'The wife left me a long, long time ago and who blames her, right son?' I was about to fucking hang myself with my headset."

"You should be used to those types by now. They keep us paid."

"Paid and laid! Am I right?" He was still laughing up at the stars when Leah honked from the street.

She really does love driving. I slid onto the leather seat and turned the "butt warmer" on. I love her driving too.

"You're such a kid. It's June! You just like pushing buttons." She leaned over to give me a swift peck on my cheek.

"I've told you, it's comfy! Now it feels like Christmas in here. You should make gingerbread."

"I need to stop by the bakery for a minute, k?"

"Only if we can have a quickie on the counter." She didn't laugh. "Fine, no quickie, as long as you want, the whole enchilada!" Still no reaction. "Baby?"

"Sorry, I'm just distracted."

"What's wrong?" I slid my hand around her thigh.

She sighed as I felt the familiar bump-bump of Sprinkles On Top's driveway. I loved how everything was just a stop light and a bump-bump away from each other here.

"Come inside, we need to talk."

Unlocking the door seemed to take hours while I replayed every novel scene that evolved after those four words: we need to talk. But I would have never even dreamed that her cousin had found "the perfect little spot" in Manhattan. I'm sure they don't even have call centers up there.

"You'll find something to do," she'd pleaded.

"But I don't want to find something to do, I already have

something to do."

"I promise you'll like it there."

"I like it here."

She cried; I rested my hands on the crepe display case.

"Well, I signed the lease."

I thought about what would happen if someone ever called me to do a survey. I thought about what my voice would sound like. The silence of the background. Not like the people I call who say "No" and hang up. I would take the survey. I would choke out "Single" when asked my marital status.

"Can you take me home please?" I asked, like a little boy scared to spend the night at his best friend's house.

And she did, sniffling but still tapping her fingers to her favorite Oldies station. I missed her already.

"Told you," Aileen had said. "You can do better. Do you know how many thefts there are up there? And rats, dear Lord. Besides, you can't just leave me here."

And I knew she was right, again, as always. I was probably meant to live with my sister forever, competing in whose life was worse. But I was comfortable.

"Maybe we should get a cat."

Aileen snorted and replied, "I don't know. Maybe just a hamster?"

"Okay."

I'd never be comfortable in a taxi or subway or in the bright lights of Times Square. I could see bright lights and it hurt.

Everyone was rooting for us (except Aileen I guess).

But I failed. Leah moved to the city, Aileen's candle finally fell to a puddle and the wick, and my sheets no longer smelled like snickerdoodle.

It took me three years. I finally realized that she was worth it. She had always been worth it, but I was just so scared.

So I packed up everything I'd ever owned, which wasn't much, and paid for Aaron to help me get to New York and find Leah.

I thought about finding what station she used most often and waiting right by the stairs, sunglasses on, trying desperately to play the violin. But I really just wanted to hug her and hold her and apologize. And besides, where would I ever find a cheap violin?

"Man, are you sure you wanna go through with this? This is some hard shit, trying to not let people run into you."

"People who can see are still running into each other. It's normal."

"Yeah, I guess you're right."

I bought a bouquet of flowers on the way, asked Aaron how I looked ("Same as always, dude."), and went over what I wanted to say in my head.

The city was mostly what I had expected. I didn't hear any people screaming "RATS!" like Aileen made it sound. And no one tried to steal from us. It didn't smell that great, especially in the subway, but that changed when we were in front of her shop. It smelled just like her shop back home—I could almost picture every item laid out, selling fast.

"Do you see her?"

"Nope. Should I go to the front of the line and ask?"

"Um...yeah. Let's both go." Then I understood why Aaron wanted to go alone. It was a madhouse. People yelled at us because they thought we were cutting.

"There's a line, sir," the girl at the counter said sourly.

"I'm just looking for Leah."

"Leah...?"

"The owner."

"Oh. Uh...ok, one sec."

And then I finally heard her voice.

"Oh my god, Luke?"

"Hi. I'm sorry it took me so long. I don't know what I was thinking-"

"Let's step outside. Michelle, call me if you need anything." I realized that everyone behind me was probably staring and listening. I felt embarrassed. I was that guy with his hands in his pockets, looking around, lost.

Aaron said he was off to "explore" and to call him when me and Leah were "square."

She took me to the nearby Central Park, just like she'd always talked about. But we weren't holding hands. The fresh air was a great change. I felt more at ease.

"Are you...are you seeing someone?"

"No."

"Can you ever forgive me?"

"I don't know."

I grabbed her hand, which I knew would be resting on

her knee. "Can you please try? I'll do whatever it takes. I'm so sorry, baby."

"Are you just tired of living with Aileen?"

I laughed. "Well, yes. But that's not why I'm here. I've been wanting to be here since the minute you left."

"Well then why didn't you come sooner? A lot can happen in three years."

"I know. And it has. I'm so proud of you—for doing this. I just wish I could've been here to support you. I was just so scared—of the city, of losing you…I love you so much."

She was quiet for a long time.

"I love you too."

And the rest, as they say, is history.

I got a great job, *not* at a call center. Leah's one shop became three shops, which then expanded to one in L.A. and one in D.C. She was running around like the happiest madwoman alive and I was keeping her sane. I loved it.

And then we decided to have children. Leah was almost 36 and she wasn't sure if her body would give in. But we wanted a kid more than anything in the world. It seemed to be the only thing missing from our near-perfect lives.

We had an amazing apartment, we both loved our jobs, we had a lovable Seeing Eye dog named Max, and all the dessert we could ever want.

"What if the baby's blind?" I asked her one day. She was three months pregnant. I was scared shitless.

"It doesn't matter, Luke."

"But it does."

"Not to me."

Rachel turned out perfect though. She was happy and beautiful and she slept through the entire night. What more could we ask for?

We lived long, sweet-as-pie lives. We spoiled Rachel rotten, even when she had kids of her own (that we spoiled even more). And we even did what Leah had always said we would—we saved up and traveled, everywhere. We were the typical tourists, except worse because Leah would loudly (out of excitement) describe every building and every view and every dish and well, everything to me in full detail.

"It's like Christmas morning, birthday cake, and Thanksgiving dinner all rolled in one and sprinkled on top of a city," she'd said, breathless, about Venice.

I soaked in her wonder and never told her that I got more happiness from that than the actual travel. The way her voice sounded—so amazed, ready to explode with joy. The way her laugh was filled with more pleasure than it ever had been before. The way we made love—two grandparents on a beach in Mykonos. It was pure bliss.

But when she was 73, she had a stroke. I was left with pictures that I could only hold and a freezer full of microwavable dinners. An old man and his dog, both waiting for death.

Her shop became so popular that cookbooks were published every year, never available in Braille. Not that I'd ever attempt to bake. I made do listening on the edge of my seat, to Aileen or Aaron read the instructions aloud, hoping to hear "I miss you" somewhere in between three eggs and one tablespoon of baking soda. Anything that referenced me, us.

Only "Enjoy!" at the end of every recipe, and I smiled, tasting each dessert perfectly, remembering how she licked the crumbs from my fingertips.

CHAPTER 4

The whole watching through a window wasn't a strange concept to me. It just comes naturally. It's what we all picture—being able to watch your loved ones. Most people probably picture looking from a cloud or something. Something more glamorous or mystical than through a giant window. But whatever.

I watched my husband and my daughter and my grandchildren and my bakeries—out of eyes that they wouldn't even recognize. I was Nina and Leah: Nina with the memory of Leah. I struggled with this, sure that I'd forget one of the lives, scared that it'd be Leah's, and therefore I wouldn't be able to watch anymore.

But I didn't feel disconnected. I felt more whole than I ever had. Full of life. I thought about the strangeness of not only growing up in two different places and decades (although my second life only started a decade before my first) but also—living as two different races. I kept looking down at my hands, not really knowing what I'd see, but my lightly tanned skin remained. Leah had been dark almond. This must be what God feels like, I thought, and then started laughing.

"Um, Nina?" I hadn't even noticed Ruth walking up behind me. "I just remembered this." She held out a faded, folded sheet of paper.

I started crying. "Thank you so much, Ruth." I marveled for a second at how she hadn't changed a bit. Maybe a little more tired looking, but that was to be expected.

"I'll give you some privacy. I hope you'll tell me everything later."

"Of course. Thank you." Poor Ruth. She was probably dying with curiosity. I'd appeared in the room and just about given her a heart attack. The only thing I told her before I rushed to the window was, "Yes, we were together." Technically, I didn't know that. Luke could've just been Luke, someone else's old husband. But he wasn't; I could feel it in my bones.

I stole a glance at Luke and Max II. They were still listening to reruns of "The Andy Griffith Show". Then I read the short note at least a hundred times.

Dear Nina,

I was thinking. Maybe one day we'll find a way to live together and die together, wouldn't that be something? I mean, anything's possible, obviously. Start brainstorming, baby. And thanks for waiting. I love you more than all the love in all the waiting rooms combined with all the love on earth…and combined with any other love anywhere else!

Love,

Jude

He *would* give me homework after I die, I thought. Live together and die together? This coming from the guy who thinks this is all some sort of "systematic error"? Crazy man.

I stuck the note in my pocket, noticing that these were *my* jeans, Nina's jeans: jeans Leah wished she could fit into. I needed paper.

I walked over to the desk, grabbed a pen and a notepad, and walked back to the window. Ruth opened her mouth and then closed it. I felt bad, but I didn't feel any huge obligation to her. Jude was the one who spent fifty years getting to know her.

I started scribbling. I made two columns: Nina and Leah. I compared everything from physical characteristics to family and friends and morals and fears. Physically, we were entirely different, almost opposites. Morally or ethically or whatever you want to call it, we were extremely similar. Besides the fact that Leah was Christian and I didn't believe in God until I died. We both loved poetry. We both fell in love, hard and fast, without holding back. I think we would have been friends, probably best friends.

Our families were both very loving with high expectations of us our entire lives. But other than that, they were opposites. Leah's dad was a preacher; my dad was in the Coast Guard. Leah had four siblings, I had none. I started comparing Jude and Luke. I'd almost filled five pages so far.

I thought about how, if people could remember all their lives, all the time, judgment would quite possibly be erased. If you've lived as a black woman *and* a white woman, why would you ever be racist? If you knew what it was like to be blind or overweight, really *knew* what it was like, imagine the difference in compassion you'd have for others. A world where everyone was truly understanding and equal. It was bizarre to think about. But maybe you're only "allowed" to "alter" in your next life if you were already...well, if you weren't racist to begin with. The only way to really know is if I found someone who was extremely prejudiced in the waiting room, and asked them about all their lives. But Jude was white both times, and he's not racist at all.

I scribbled away, my mind racing. I wrote down every theory and question. And then I remembered something.

"Hey, Ruth!" I called out, not willing to get up from my brainstorming bubble.

"Yes?" She'd walked over and seemed irritated. Jude probably built me up and here I was, some bitch ignoring her for three hours.

"I was just wondering, did you change the handbook?"

"What do you mean?" But I could tell she knew exactly what I was referring to.

"Jude's note to you. I read it."

"Oh, that. No, the handbook is the same."

"Why?"

"There was no reason to change it."

"But people need to know!"

"Nina, there is nothing to know. It's been over 70 years and Jude is still the only person who's waited."

"Well now there are two people."

Ruth looked me up and down. "We don't know that.

You've only been here a few hours."

I glared at her. "Seriously? And how many other people in this room have been here as long as me?"

She rolled her eyes. "Even so, you and Jude are obvious exceptions. It's not like you are two people who aren't connected at all. You practically count as one individual. And I'm not going to change the whole handbook just because one individual didn't exactly go by the rules."

"But you don't have to change the whole handbook. Just add a section. Or even a paragraph for God's sake. I'll even write it for you." I was starting to get pissed off.

"You just think it's so easy, that it's not a big deal at all."

"It's not! It's necessary!"

"Have you even thought about the consequences? Do you have any idea how people will react? It'll be a mess. And who will have to clean it up? Not you. Not Jude. Me."

I was silent. I knew she was right, but at the same time...I thought about medicine and side effects and how if something bad happened to one person, the company had to print that possibility on their commercials and bottles...

My voice softened. "I guess I'd just like to think that we live in a world of full disclosure. A democracy in life and in death. If something significant, something huge happens to one of us, I just think it's a divine right for everyone to know. People are going to go on for the rest of time, thinking they're alone when they die, never to be reunited again with their loved ones. But maybe it doesn't have to be that way. Maybe this is some kind of experiment or test. To see how people react. To see if it's worth it to let us be with the people we love most, forever."

Ruth stared at me, blinking. Then she glanced down at her list. "Damnit. Danita Ford! Jessie Altenhoff! Linh Le!" She looked back at me. "Well I see that you and Jude are both stubborn as hell, not to mention distracting." The corner of her mouth twitched.

"Yes. It makes for some great fighting and making up." I smiled and touched the glass subconsciously.

"Well. All I can say is, I'll think about it."

"But haven't you been thinking about it the past 70 years?"

"No. Not at all. People are upset enough here. Why make things worse?"

"But don't you see? It would make everything better."

She blinked at me again and cocked her head a little bit. "How about this: you write it all up and I'll read it and see what I think."

"I'll take it!"

Ruth started to walk away, shaking her head. But then she turned back and said, "Oh, and Nina?"

"Yeah?"

"This isn't some apple in a tree, waiting to see if someone will take a bite."

"Well this is *not* just a glitch or coincidence. Why would anyone do that?"

"Why would there be an 'anyone'? And of all the people that person would choose, do you really think it would be you and Jude?"

I didn't know whether to be offended or honest. I mean, I know we're not the best of the best, but I thought that was kind of the point. If this was some sort of test for the average human being, I'd say we fit the standards. "But there has to be a reason."

"Why does everyone think that about everything? It's just a silly comfort to think that. A security blanket."

She called out more names, on the way back to her desk. I wanted to shout at her, "No it isn't you old, lonely hag! It's the truth! Everything happens for a reason!" And then I realized how young and stupid that sounded.

I woke up with my forehead sticking to the window, surrounded by balled up papers. I yawned and checked on Luke. He was sitting by my grave, talking away. I'd spent the last few days scribbling more ideas and notes for my handbook addition. I'd stayed awake almost the entire time, barely talked to the employees who tried to introduce themselves, and now I'd slept through my own funeral. Aileen was there. She was trying to convince him to move back to Alabama, so she could take care of him like she used to. Well, so that they could be taken care of together. She lived in a retirement home.

"I don't need you anymore!" He'd yelled at her. "This is where Leah is!"

"She's not here anymore, Luke..." They'd never looked more like twins than at that moment: both sad-eyed and wrinkly, bald spots peeking out of their short, white hair.

"Yes she is! And I'm not leaving her! I'll die soon too and then we'll be together!"

I'd cried and thought, *if he only knew*. I prayed that he'd at least take our daughter's offer to go and live with her, but I knew he wouldn't. I knew he was just waiting for death, and doing anything he could to speed up the process.

It was strange watching him, an old man becoming senile. I knew that I had just been around his age, but now I felt so young, so full of the memories that had been fading away. How bizarre, to remember when you couldn't remember.

I picked up the notebook by my side and started writing about age and memories and brain capacity and how in the waiting room, all of that stops being science and starts being this whole new...experience. I wanted to get all my ideas out before I started writing whatever it was that I wanted people to know. The truth was that I could've written a novel. But I knew Ruth would only "publish" something short and sweet, to the point.

How could you be short and sweet about something like this though? This wasn't a recipe in one of my cookbooks or homework instructions for my class. I couldn't just be like, "Oh hey, by the way, there *has* been one case where two random people's names weren't called until they both died, and a spot was found for them to live another life together."

I suddenly noticed someone standing over me.

"Um, hi, I'm Donna, we kind of met earlier. I was just, um, wondering if maybe you'd like to sleep in the break room or over here by the desk? It's just that, um, Ruth told me to make sure you were 'discreet' and to tell people that you worked here if they asked. And, well, I thought that you sleeping by the window would be ok for a little while, but now people are pointing and staring and talking and someone just asked me about you. So...yeah."

I smiled at the nervous girl. She looked so young. I wondered why she was "chosen." Jude had told me about Joe committing suicide, but it was hard to picture this girl wanting to end her life—so early.

"Hi, Donna. Sure, no problem. And sorry for being in my own world over here. I have a lot on my mind. If you want, I can tell you about it."

"Um, yeah, that'd be great. Ruth wouldn't tell me very much." She rolled her eyes and I grinned, gathering up my papers. She was watching me with wonder and I felt bad for her because I knew what she was thinking. She was thinking I was some kind of miracle or angel or guardian or god. That might sound conceited but I don't mean it like that. But what would you think if you've been working in purgatory for a while, watching thousands of people come and go, and then some woman arrives who just stays, waiting. She didn't think I was a glitch, I can tell you that much. Most people believe in purpose when it presents itself with such...promise.

I could see that she was definitely right about the people watching me. There were ugly glares coming from all directions.

"I've never seen anyone sleep in here before," Donna said shyly.

"Well, I'm guessing you've never seen anyone stay here this long?"

"Nope. There was a boy last month who was here for an hour and I thought that was amazing. I hardly ever get to talk to anyone since they're always in and out. Plus, the little time that they *are* here, they're usually staring out the window. It was nice to get to talk to that boy, to actually learn his name before it came up on the list and I had to call it and watch him leave." She stared at the door wistfully.

"This guy sounds cute."

She laughed and laughed. "He was."

"He must have been a really interesting person to have taken that long to get placed."

"Funny that you say that, 'cause most people take the same amount of time. It makes you wonder, really. I mean, I don't see why it would've taken that long for him. He was probably one of the nicest guys I've ever met and I guess that's rare. No one that attractive has ever talked to me for that long. But I hope being nice isn't rare enough to make it hard to place someone because of it."

"Nah, no way is that possible. I'm still here and it's not because I'm a saint." I liked this girl; she gave me more theories and ideas. I was itching to start writing again. But I was thankful to have someone who seemed just as interested as me in talking about this place.

"Why *are* you here?"

"Well..." And then I told her everything.

She was silent the entire time. I looked at her after I finished, waiting for some sort of response.

"I knew this would happen one day. I was just kind of

hoping it'd be to me."

That was not the response I was expecting. But then *she* explained why *she* was here.

"I pegged this whole thing. I dreamed it, I thought about it, I believed in it, I wrote about it. It feels like this place is straight out of my head. Sometimes I wonder if it's even real or if I'm just wrapped up in my own world, but really in some asylum somewhere pounding my head against a padded wall. And all of you are just figments of my imagination. Or even worse, what if it's like that John Cusack movie, what's it called? Where the whole time, you think they're all separate people, but in the end, it turns out they're all just different personalities."

She talked fast and she talked a lot. But I didn't mind. Under the circumstances, I didn't want to waste any time either. I wanted to know it all, lay it all out on the table. I felt like I was on the brink of some huge discovery that would change mankind forever. But I guess that was a little impossible since everyone, including myself, forgets everything after stepping through that door.

"Donna, are you saying that you had some kind of vision?"

"No, no, no. I just always had my own idea about what happens after death. And this was my idea. Reincarnation. With a twist I guess. And apparently, I was spot on. Maybe the only person ever to be spot on."

"That can't be the reason you were chosen. There has to be others who have thought about this before."

"This isn't my first life though. I believed in this hundreds of years ago. I'm sure there are others now, maybe. I don't know, I guess it's kind of hard to explain."

I was staring wide-eyed at her now: she was the amazement. "So do you think that everything, to a tee, that you thought is fact? Like, is there a God?"

She laughed and played with her stringy brown hair. "I don't know. Working here doesn't exactly give me all the answers like I thought it would. I think faith is never really answered like people think it will be. Because that's the point of faith—believing with no proof."

She still sounded nervous and unsure, but her words were so profound. She was right—that made perfect sense. But I felt bad for the hundreds of thousands of people out there expecting to meet God. I wondered how many people lost faith in the waiting room. And then did they gain it back in their next life? Or did they lose it forever? Death was horrifying for everyone except Jude and me I thought. But I guess that's arguable. I mean, you do get another shot at doing what you always wanted but never did, etcetera, etcetera. But then again, what if you just keep living life after life after life—all without doing what you want or finding true love or real happiness or any other mushy gushy bullshit. What if you never reach your potential or follow your dream or accomplish anything? Wouldn't this whole thing just be more of a punishment? Or is Life, no matter how it's lived, still a blessing? That's hard for me to believe. Leah got everything she'd ever wanted. But me? The love of my life died after we'd only been married a few years. I never published a great novel or edited a great novel. I would've been happy with just one of those. But I did teach English for over 40 years total. I guess that's something. I taught a few students who went on to do the things I'd wanted to do. It was a good life. Not perfect at all, but long and happy for the most part.

I could barely hear Donna calling out names from her list. I blinked hard, realizing I'd been daydreaming, my eyebrows furrowed together, and staring hard at a pencil on the desk.

"Sorry," I said sheepishly. "What were we talking about?"

"Don't worry about it. It's a lot to take in. For me too."

"So do you...believe in God?"

"People sure to bring him up a lot in here and I can understand why but, on the other hand, why does he even have to be a part of this? This could just be something entirely separate. Or it could be like Earth—which some people thinks he plays a huge role in and some people think he just supervises from time to time. I don't think he has everything laid out in a perfect little plan, I think we all make impacts and change things and shake the world up a bit. Whenever I pictured this place, it wasn't some kind of heaven. It was just another step in the process, something that had to be done. Maybe he made you wait here, maybe he didn't. But either way, he's not controlling every little move you make."

"So you do believe in him then?" I couldn't wait to tell Jude. Because obviously, I was right. This girl was some kind of prophet; anything she believed was obviously fact.

"Well I don't know if I'd say that. I just believe in *something*, that's all. It's hard to believe there's *nothing* out there."

I sighed loudly, letting my head fall into my palm.

"Sorry to disappoint." She laughed.

"It's just ridiculous to think that there are never any answers. I mean, how depressing is that? No matter what we do, we'll never know anything of real importance."

"I wouldn't say that. I think it's just a matter of putting everything into perspective. You can't say that death and God and heaven are the most important things because then, what meaning would life have?"

"You're very philosophical for being so young."

"Well I'm a Philosophy major." We laughed.

"That explains a lot. I'm glad we can talk about this stuff though. Jude had a hard time when he was here. No one was all that interested in the 'whys' and the 'what ifs'. He went a little crazy thinking about everything on his own. And then when I finally met him, we didn't have enough time to talk about everything."

"I've felt the same way. I try to talk to Ruth, since she obviously has a lot of experience here...but she won't say much of anything. And the handbook? Give me a break. That thing is worthless."

"Funny you should bring that up." I grinned and explained my plan, gesturing to all the crumpled up papers.

"So *that's* what you were doing."

"Yes. And I felt like I was going insane. So maybe you're my sanity being handed back to me."

"I don't know about that..."

"But you'll help me?"

"Of course. Anything to prove Ruth wrong."

We spent the rest of her shift writing and planning and philosophizing and laughing like two women who had been friends for years. All we needed was a good bottle of wine.

ۯڒ

Donna definitely answered a lot of questions for me. I told her she was my guardian angel and we laughed about it, but I was 100 percent serious. She was just as curious about the race and all around ethics questions, so we started "interviewing" willing participants.

Donna said she'd been "every color under the sun." This confirmed my guardian angel belief. We talked to a lot of people who said the exact same thing. But we talked to even more people who had been the same race every single time.

"Who knows if it really means anything," Donna said. "I mean think about it. If there is a God, and he wanted to tackle racism, wouldn't he keep the non-judgmental people the same race over and over again, until they convinced everyone else in their race?"

"That makes no sense and perfect sense at the same time," I said.

Our interviews basically proved nothing. Only that everyone had a different story. We quickly realized that while "interviewing" was fun and extremely interesting, it was getting us nowhere.

So we stuck to writing. I told her about Jude and our lives, she told me about her lives.

And we were done polishing our finished product in a few months. We thought about Ruth the whole time: what she wouldn't want to be said, what she would actually approve of.

When Ruth came in for her shift the next day, we were anxiously waiting at the desk. She glared at us and sighed, holding out her hand.

"Before you read it, we'd like to just explain a little."

"Go ahead."

I nodded at Donna. We'd agreed that Ruth liked her more. Not much more, but more.

"Well, we've talked to a lot of people passing through— don't worry, we haven't told them anything about what we're doing. But we've realized that we're not the only ones who have different theories. We heard hundreds of ideas about this place, about life and death, heaven and hell, religion and aliens, the devil and evolution, reincarnation and dreams and comas and drug highs and insane asylums and magic and government conspiracies…you name it, we've heard it as a theory."

Ruth raised an eyebrow. She looked bored. Of course she'd heard this all before, I was sure. She'd been here for hundreds of years. Jude was the only thing that had ever surprised or baffled her. But we had to find a way to get through to her.

"So, instead of just writing an insert for the handbook, which hardly any people read, we thought we'd make an entirely separate publication. And instead of just writing about the possibility of me and Jude's situation, we wrote about a lot of possibilities."

Ruth's face was getting a little red. She opened her mouth and Donna quickly cut her off.

"Why present one idea when there are so many? Who's to say that our lives follow the rules of the handbook precisely? Nina and Jude didn't. Nothing's set in stone. And I think people will see this as a huge relief. What we've written is not only informative and educational, but some of it is just downright entertaining. And maybe that's what this place needs. Some lightheartedness about our situation."

"And maybe that's why me and Jude came around in the first place. Not simply to shake up your world. But to fill some kind of void, to attach that missing puzzle piece. Maybe that's why you're still here, Ruth." My voice softened. "You've done an amazing job keeping things in order, but maybe the world needs more than just order. What we've written…it'll give people so much more than just hope about finding loved ones…"

"It'll give them understanding. About themselves, about others. And most importantly, about the fact that this place doesn't mean you have to drop your beliefs. This is just another forum for you to believe whatever the hell you want. This room should be about optimism, but it's not, no one is happy here. Maybe this will change that."

Donna looked at me meaningfully. But I really had nothing else to say.

"So…read it, think about it please. And let us know what you decide." I handed her the papers.

Ruth was silent, calm. That worried me. She sat down and began reading, handing Donna the list of names waiting to be called.

We sat nervously for almost three hours, taking turns calling names, and glancing at Ruth every five seconds. It seemed like she read each page five times before moving onto the next.

I was going over every single word I'd written, wondering what she would omit. I smiled thinking about our Quotes section.

"Haven't you all seen the finale of Lost? This is just part of my made-up in-between world. I'll be movin' along soon, to where I'm really supposed to be."
–Ed Michaels, Adams, TN

"I think I've been with my husband, Greg, in every life. Just because we never see each other in here—that doesn't mean anything."
–Reyna Campos, Mobile, AL

"Just ride the wave, baby. That's all I can really say." –Jake Reynolds, Key West, FL

"I think when you get to the right life, the one you were really meant for, that's your last. I can't wait till that day. The day I'll never see this room again."
–Colton Licalzi, Buda, TX

It was…inspiring to hear everyone's opinion, to know that they still had ideas and beliefs and hopes and dreams and all that mushy gushy stuff that I thought death killed in people. It made everyone seem so…alive. I felt alive. Like I was working toward something. I would've still felt alive though—knowing I was waiting for Jude. But all these other people that we got quotes from? What reason did they have? I mean, sure, there were quotes we purposefully left out that could be summarized to say, "Fuck it all". But for the most part, people were optimistic about this whole ordeal. They either thought the whole process was amazing or they thought this was a step leading to something more amazing.

I looked at Donna. She was deep in thought as well. I wondered if we were thinking the same thing. Probably. She'd told me one day that we were "very similar souls."

I heard Ruth clear her throat and my eyes jumped to hers. She motioned for us to come back to the desk. She looked...stern. She always looked that way. This is never going to happen, I thought.

"Alright, let's do it." She tapped her nails on the packet.

Donna's mouth was hanging open. I couldn't seem to speak either.

"Well? All of that and the two of you have nothing to say? Finally, I've silenced the beast!"

We looked at each other's gaping faces and started to laugh. And then we hugged Ruth until she said, "Ok, ok, enough!" and shooed us away. "You have work to do."

We edited and printed copies in less than two days. Ruth even agreed to email "the addition," as she called it, to the other waiting rooms' managers.

I was finally a published author. And it felt great. If only Jude could have been there to see the effect it had on people.

But I only had to wait another three months, and there he was.

❧

I was in the middle of explaining "my situation" to an older woman named Lorena, who said she'd read the explanation in the handbook but she was still confused.

"It's just that you didn't say what you did on earth, when you were alive, that was so great. Were you the one who found the cure to cancer, honey?"

I blinked at her. She was dead serious.

"No ma'am. We didn't do anything special—" And then I saw Luke out of the corner of my eye. He was smiling at me, his wrinkles slowly smoothing out into Jude's dimples.

By the time he caught me in his arms, he was Jude entirely: no more hunched back, age spots, or glazed over eyes.

"It's so good to see you, to actually see you," he whispered, crying softly.

"Honey, is that him?" I heard Lorena call from her seat. I laughed into his neck.

"Of course it's you." I kissed his neck.

"Is that a new friend?" he asked, pulling away and looking at me in a way he never had.

"Kind of. I've been busy. There's so much to tell you. I feel horrible for not…seeing that you passed."

"Baby, I don't blame you if you've never looked out that window once. All I did after you died was sit with Max. Just sitting—in front of the TV, in front of your grave, at the kitchen table—just sitting. That's how I died. That's all." He touched my nose, lips, hair.

"Why are you looking at me like that? You're making me blush."

"Now I understand what you meant last time, when you felt so strange and amazing being young again. Plus, I'd forgotten what beauty looked like. No matter how many times you described yourself and our surroundings to me, there's just no comparison to this...*this*." He motioned around the room with a huge grin on his face.

I felt an unreal surge of happiness. I thought back to when I first realized that I was madly in love with him. We were in a restaurant, eating side salads, enjoying each other's company in silence. He suddenly announced, "You know, my favorite part is the croutons," looking at the one on his fork and then crunching away. I have no idea why, but at that moment, I knew I was going to marry that man.

And then I saw Donna nearly running towards us.

"You're Jude!" She hugged him almost as vigorously as I had.

"That I am," he said awkwardly, halfway hugging her back while still holding my hand.

"Sorry—I'm Donna, I work here. I've heard so much about you. Did she tell you about the addition yet?" Ruth called it that so much that it kind of stuck, unfortunately.

"He *just* got here, Donna." I gave her a significant look.

"Oh. Right. You should step into the back for a bit to, uh, catch up. I mean, people are staring."

I smiled graciously and led a very quiet Jude to the break room.

"Nice to meet you, Donna," he called out softly before closing the door behind him.

"Are you shell-shocked or something?" I giggled and nibbled on his ear.

"I've just never felt this way before. I feel so...so..."

"Happy?"

"Lucky. We're so lucky."

"I know." And we kissed and kissed and kissed until a familiar knocking filled the room.

"Jude? Jude? I came as fast as I could! Jude!"

We gave each other a knowing look. Mine was probably more of an annoyed look.

"Come in, Ruth, we're not naked yet," he called fondly, which annoyed me more. She burst into the room and the look on her face was like a mother seeing her long lost son.

"It's been so long!" They embraced, swaying back and forth. Was she seriously crying? I saw Donna peeking into the room curiously. We locked eyes and I rolled mine. She stifled a laugh.

"How've you been? Have you kept my wife company?"

Ruth wiped a tear away and smiled grimly. "I think Donna's been doing most of that." Jude looked at me and raised an eyebrow. "Have they told you about the addition yet? According to the note you left me a century ago, you'll be very happy."

"They haven't had a chance, but I'm dying to know what the hell everyone's talking about."

So we told him, all three of us taking turns—Ruth's voice sarcastic and cynical but yielding, Donna's was ecstatic, mine proud.

Jude beamed when I handed him a copy. I was reminded of Luke's smile when he first held our daughter.
There's that one smile that everyone has hidden in their
back pocket, that's only taken out on special occasions.
Watching him read through it, I smiled mine.

"Who would've thought that I'd never go down in history for anything during either of my lives…but in death?
In death, my name is in print. In death, I've done something no other dead man has ever done before. In death,
I am a legend." He pumped out his chest like a superhero
and we all laughed.

But it was true. Our names were already becoming
widely discussed in the waiting room. A very prominent
CNN reporter even interviewed me the other day. When I
reminded him gently that he was dead and that this story
would never be broadcasted, he winked and said, "How
do you know?"

I told Jude about this later and admitted that I felt so
guilty because I was undeniably disappointed that the reporter was the most famous person I'd met or even seen.

"I know it's wrong, but I'm jealous of you. You met
Oprah *and* Obama. It's not fair." I felt like stomping my
foot and crossing my arms to complete my childish rant.

Jude laughed so hard that he started wheezing, an effect
that I'd only witnessed a few times in our first life, one
being when his old roommate farted during a Chemistry
final. The entire class stared in the direction of the fart
awkwardly. A few people snickered. But Jude? He was
red-faced and wheezing, barely recovering in time to

finish the rest of his exam. Naturally, everyone thought he was the fart culprit.

"Baby—I didn't meet them! I was too nervous to actually go up to either of them. Other people were swarming them anyway."

"Still."

"Plus, you've probably met people of the same caliber and just not known it."

"What do you mean?"

"I doubt every famous person's happiest life is their famous one. Think about it—the drugs, the failed marriages, the bad press... I wouldn't choose that. For all you know, you've talked to the entire cast of the Ocean's movies."

I thought about that for a minute. "Good point. I like that."

"Except for maybe Brad Pitt. I think he'd come here as Brad Pitt." He stroked his chin. I giggled and punched his arm lightly.

All four of us had inevitably started a debate about the effect of "the addition." It mainly felt like three-against-one, but we all admitted that Ruth brought up valid points. For example, the undeniable truth that no matter what people learn or experience while they're in this room, they'll never remember in life.

"Therefore, it really doesn't even matter—none of it. I didn't even have to write a packet at all. Earth will go on in the exact same fashion as it would if this place didn't exist. It's pointless, really. I think it will go out of fashion like anything else that is deemed unnecessary."

"But who do you think gets to deem it unnecessary?" Donna's eyebrows wiggled.

"Who knows, child. Us? Maybe when the right number of people all agree that this place sucks, we'll just evaporate. Maybe you three are the last straws, holding on for dear life to this deathly room."

We all looked at her, a little worried. She was so old, so fragile looking. The spark her eyes had when I'd first met her was gone. She used to believe this place, her job, was so important. She thought she kept the world running smoothly, a goddess with a nametag. Now she realized the truth: that she'd been kept alive to keep the waiting room—not the world—running smoothly. And she saw it as an absolute waste. She was right about the fact that she'd stopped aging. I just hope she got the chance to die soon. How morbid and awful that sounds! And I know Jude doesn't feel the same. She keeps him sane, in a way. She's the only constant here. But death is what she needs. We all need it.

"Well if we're the last straws, then it's staying that way! There's no way you'd ever convince me that this place is a waste." Jude got up and squeezed Ruth, kissing her on the cheek. He treated her just like he treated his mom, who I missed just as much now as I did the day she died.

You wouldn't think your mind or body could hold so much emotion: the loss of loved ones from not one, but two lives. But you'd be surprised. It's like your brain and heart and skin stretches when it needs to. You learn quickly in the waiting room that in this stage of uncertainty and window-watching, you can handle anything. Wouldn't that be nice to have when you're alive?

It had been six hours this time. Donna had fallen asleep at the desk and Ruth looked like she was about to follow suit.

"It's time, my love." I whispered in Jude's ear, showing him our names in print. He turned my palms up and kissed them, slowly.

It's funny how the brain works. How it decides to pop random memories into your head unexpectedly. I had a flashback to our first year of dating, lying in my dorm room bed. He suddenly had said, "Do you wear Secret deodorant?" I looked at him like he was crazy. "Um, yes. Why?" I didn't usually talk to people about deodorant, especially people I'd just made out with. "I just recognized the scent. My mom wears Secret." I started laughing and teasing him. Who says something like that? I smiled, reminiscing, and Jude's voice and kisses brought me back to our version of reality.

"I miss you. I want to find you when we're still in diapers this time. So we can be together longer." He kissed each of my fingertips.

"Well maybe we will, darling."

And just like that, we did.

Deb & Blair

She remembered when she'd kissed him in the sand-box when they were five. And when she and her friend Mallory from down the street, held a wedding ceremony in her backyard when they were seven, forcing Blair to walk her up the playset, holding her hand. Mallory had slicked his hair down with water from the sprinkler and said, "You better be a great husband to Deb. Now I marry you. Slide down the slide!"

They slid down, still holding hands. Deb was giggling. She remembered feeling so happy. Blair was just an awkward little boy who unfortunately, didn't live near a single boy from school. He'd lived next door to Deb his entire life; she was his best friend. But marry her? Already? Oh well, he thought, I guess she's as good as any wife.

When his mom found two of her rings missing, and found one in his pocket while doing laundry, they had a "meeting" with Deb and *her* mom. Both women wore floral dresses with bright red lipstick. Deb and Blair both remembered them as carbon copies of each other, except one was blonde and the other brunette. They had tea and pie and stifled their laughter the entire time, while trying to explain to the two best friends that they couldn't get married until they were much older.

"Like next year, when we're eight?" Deb asked.

"No, sweetie." The mothers exchanged amused looks. "Closer to ten years from now."

Deb started counting down. She wanted a big, white, pretty dress with lace. Lots of lace.

"Should we stop letting them spend so much time

together?" Deb's mom whispered later.

"No, for God's sake, they're only seven. Who knows what we'll do when they're older though. And whatever you do, don't tell your husband!" This echoed a few years back when the pair was caught "showing each other what their private areas looked like."

Pearl Street was a perfect 1950s set-up: green lawns, picket fences, bike riding and sidewalk strolling all day. They had an amazing childhood together: inseparable, as most people observed. Even when they turned 13 and the mothers began trying to distance them, they stuck like glue. They'd make plans on the school bus of how to sneak around their parents. Most of these plans involved sliding through windows after bedtime.

That was the summer he kissed her.

"That was much better than the sandbox," she'd said, breathless. He turned bright pink and couldn't seem to speak for a long time. She giggled and twirled her hair.

"You know," he said, when he could finally talk, "the first memory I have is of you."

She smiled. "Me too. Of you."

She's absolutely, positively the most beautiful thing on the planet, he thought. "Mine is of you, sitting on your mom's lap, staring at me, sitting on *my* mom's lap. You had pigtails and pink ribbons and I don't think you blinked once." They laughed, covering their mouths with their palms. The night was so quiet. "My dad would skin me alive if he caught me."

"I know." She paused. "Mine is of you, crying against the fence. I walked up and stuck my hand through and touched your hair."

He kissed her again.

And that was the year of "The School Bus Tragedy of 1960." People talked about it for years. Nowadays, teenagers put their cars in neutral on the train tracks and dust their bumpers with baby powder. They all swear to see small fingerprints after they've moved slowly to the other side of the tracks.

Eleven of the 38 had died. They'd been holding hands, their new favorite thing.

"Remember my tenth birthday party, when I cried because you started blowing out my candles?" she'd asked when he slid next to her. Her breath hung like smoke in the air, it was 34 degrees. It made her feel older and glamorous.

"How many times do I have to apologize for that? You already got me back that next year, my eleventh birthday. You dipped your finger in the icing all the way across the top of the cake! And I didn't cry!"

They laughed and started exchanging memories back and forth. They didn't care that all their other friends were making fun of them, mocking them, making smooching noises. "DEB AND BLA-AIR SITTIN' IN A TREE..." In the short but so, so sweet 14 years that they'd grown up together, they had enough memories to fill a lifetime it seemed.

And then they were gone, just like that.

There was a lot of screaming and movement. But it all happened so fast, a matter of seconds. Deb and Blair just looked at each other. He squeezed her hand, thinking about the photograph on his fridge that had been there for years. It was of the two of them, taken from behind, at a bowling alley. They both fit into one seat, his arm comfortably draped around her. They looked like a little old married couple who had spent their entire lives together, and yet, their feet couldn't even touch the floor.

CHAPTER 5

This time in the waiting room, they just held each other for hours, sobbing. It was the first time (and one of the very few to come) that they'd arrived there together, which sounded like it'd be such a joyous thing. But it wasn't.

"I really thought that would be the one. That would be the one to give all the others a run for their money." Nina's voice came out choked.

"I know, baby, me too." They cried for their families, for their friends, for all the people hurt by the tragedy. They cried for the possibilities that their lives'd had, and lost.

It took them over two hours to realize that Donna had been hovering over them, biting her nails and crying silently. She looked the same, and different. She'd gotten married and had not one, not two, but five children. Her hair was graying and wispy.

She told them about the overwhelming reaction to "the addition." Just as Ruth predicted, it caused an uproar. "What do I have to do to wait?" was the question asked daily. But just as Donna and Nina had predicted, it also comforted people in a way they never would've imagined. There were more smiles and hope filling the room than ever before. Most people thought that this meant they'd been living with their loved ones all along. Donna didn't disagree or agree with them, she just let them bask in their newfound (and very short-lived) bliss. Whereas the packets used to look untouched, they were now worn and written all over. People added their own quotes, advice, theories, and questions to every page. Donna beamed with pride and handed Nina one of the copies.

She traced over some of the scribbling with her fingers. This is my Bible, she thought, hugging it to her chest. She wished more than anything she could carry it with her into her next life.

"Also…" Donna looked hesitantly at Jude. "I'm the new manager." Ruth had finally moved on. She'd died right when she got home after her shift ended, after they'd left. That made Jude start crying again. Nina wasn't sure if they were happy tears or not. They should be, she thought.

"Just think, she could've been living in our town for all we know. She could've been your sister." His sister and brother had survived the accident. From that moment on, Jude thought of Ruth growing up and living a long, healthy life with his parents, remembering him as Blair, her favorite brother. And then dying happily, remembering him as someone completely different, but exactly the same.

Myra & Cody

It was one of those days where Myra ate a tuna fish sandwich for lunch and a tuna fish sandwich for dinner. She prepared them slowly, separately, boiling one egg at noon and another at six sharp. It had been a hard day, not a day fit for the sloppiness of spaghetti or the pickiness of potatoes. Two cans of tuna, two boiled eggs, a little squirt of mustard, and four slices of bread—life should be this simple, Myra thought. But it wasn't. There was laundry and the dentist and the cats, Peaches and Franklin. Their old neighbors had named Peaches, because of her creamy orange color. Jason named Franklin.

"Can you think of a more badass name?" They were young, contemplating moving in together after a year of dating.

"As in Benjamin?" Myra held the tiny brown thing up in front of her glasses.

"No, just Franklin. As in what-a-badass-name." He grabbed the kitten and rested it on his stomach. He loved cats, which was a confusion to Myra at first. She'd never met a man who loved cats, especially enough to adopt two of them.

"I don't know, Jason...you really want to spend your paychecks on food and litter?"

"Babe, do you know how cheap that stuff is?"

"Well what about your work? You're already distracted enough as it is, but with *two* kittens running around?"

`"It'll be fine, *Mom*."

She pushed away her doubt with words like "endearing"

and "selfless." Besides, no one had ever wanted to share something other than lunch with her. Next step, engagement, she thought.

Jason was colorful where Myra was bleak, he was funny in situations where she was awkward, he was confident everywhere, where as she was only confident in her dry cleaning and alterations shop. That's where they met. Jason was a regular, bringing in a different designer suit every couple of days, always smiling, always making Myra blush. She was average in every way. She'd never been called beautiful or ugly. She breezed by people's line of sight like a chair in a restaurant; her existence was registered but insignificant. Her hair wasn't Marilyn Monroe blonde or jet black, but something in between, like mud. Her eyes matched. Her skin wasn't flawed or flawless. She had a handful of freckles thrown over her body, but not enough to be a noticeable characteristic. No birthmark, no scars, and usually no makeup. Jason asked her out after she did the impossible—fixed a snag in his favorite tie. Silver silk Dolce. He was a lawyer who loved cats. She felt like Cinderella.

But here she was making tuna in the small studio apartment above her shop, letting the year-old Tabbies lick the cans. Jason had been long gone before their six-month check-up. She remembered smelling his cologne on their fur for a week after he left. Packed every single tie but not one kitten.

"What a dog."

That was the joke her dentist made at ten that morning

(pre-tuna of course) after Myra burst into tears and sobbed about Jason and the cats and her horrible life. It'd been almost a year and she chose *now* to break down? Of all times? Now?

She had laughed a little, mixed with sniffling sounds. "That's funny. He is. Or was. A dog I mean."

"Yeah, sounds like it. Who runs out on a perfectly good kitten?" He smiled and put a hand on her shoulder.

Myra laughed again, sounding less like an allergy attack. "*Two* perfectly good kittens!"

"Yeah, I had an ex who loved cats. I'm a dog person myself, they're just nicer animals if you ask me." He pushed his glasses up with his middle finger.

"Well you haven't met Peaches and Franklin. You'd like them." Myra caught her breath. Did she just semi-invite Dr. Morrison over to meet her cats? God, she was pathetic.

"Oh yeah? Well maybe you'll have to bring them in next time for a teeth cleaning." He smiled from under his reddish mustache. "How about we reschedule your appointment for next week? You go home and relax."

"Thanks Dr. Morrison." Myra wiped her cheeks pathetically and stood up.

"Please call me Cody."

"Ok."

And that's when she went home and made tuna.

The next week, she made sure to observe Cody's empty wedding finger. When she asked him what dry cleaner he used, he replied, "I just bought one of those fancy washing machines that does all the work for me actually."

She noticed that his shirt was a bit wrinkled and his pants looked a little faded. "Well if that ever doesn't work out, I'll give you a good deal," she said, handing him her card. Myra had a new crush. On her dentist. This is not good, she thought.

She refused to make appointments for fake toothaches or invisible cavities. It was bad enough that he had to literally put his fingers in her mouth, his lips inches from hers. Not to mention the fact that he had been witness to her first real breakdown since Jason had left.

So she just waited, crossing her fingers that he'd spill wine on his favorite button-up or buy a dry clean only blazer. Of course, she already knew that he wasn't the kind of man to buy a blazer. She liked that. He wasn't like all the Jasons that came into the shop with their precious slacks, holding them like roses or babies or hundred thousand dollar checks.

And he did come. But with empty arms.

"Cody, so nice to see you!" She got even more nervous thinking about the fact that she must sound horribly nervous. She made a mental note to start wearing mascara at least. And to never wear yoga pants to work again.

"Hi Myra." His beard looked perfectly trimmed today. "Nice shop you have here."

"Oh, thanks. I love it." She'd stood up and shaken his hand, which felt unbelievably awkward and overly formal. It's not like they ever shook hands during her appointments. But they weren't on the hugging level yet, right?

"I don't have any dry cleaning, as you can see. I was just

in the neighborhood, thought I'd drop in and make sure you were flossing." He let out an uncomfortable laugh. Was he nervous too? She felt like she was about to faint. There was nothing "in the neighborhood"…it wasn't exactly the best part of town. Next door there was a Mexican restaurant and an ancient appliance store.

She laughed at his attempted joke. "Well thanks, I feel honored. And as for the flossing, I won't lie; I just can't bring myself to put my gums through pain every day."

"So I guess it's safe to say that you'll be a bleeder again at your next checkup." He smiled; she blushed. Yeah, but not a crier, she wanted to say.

They talked for a little while, until a few customers started coming in. After the last one left, he stuck out his hand for another awkward shake. "I'll let you get back to work now."

She tried her hand at what she hoped was a sultry, seductive stare while shaking his hand. "It was great to see you, Doc." She wanted to say "Don't go!" or "Want to grab some coffee? I'll close the shop for the rest of the day!" But she didn't. He walked to the door but then suddenly turned around.

"You know, I thought about buying something fancy just so I could have an excuse to come here. But I decided against it, I thought that was pathetic. But now I realize that it's just as pathetic to say that I was in the neighborhood. Who says that? So I'm officially rewinding and saying that I came here because I wanted to see you. And I know you're not the type of woman to get a random cavity. I couldn't wait until your next checkup."

He stood at the counter, wringing his hands, flushed and a little shaky, wearing another wrinkled shirt. This is the most gorgeous man I've ever laid eyes on, Myra thought.

She walked to the door silently and flipped the open sign over.

"Well I was about to Google how to force yourself to get a cavity, to be honest."

After lunch and dinner, she felt closer to Cody than she'd ever felt to Jason. How strange, she thought, that in less than 24 hours she could develop strong feelings for someone like this... She felt connected to him, suddenly and powerfully.

Next step: meeting the cats. He loved them of course. And to wrap up a perfect day, he let her dry clean his shirt. My dentist is in my living room, on my couch, petting Franklin, shirtless. She pinched herself. Nope, this is definitely happening.

After a few glasses of Pinot, she walked him out through the shop, saying playfully, "You can bring me the rest of your wrinkly shirts whenever you'd like."

"I'll see you tomorrow then." And he kissed her and she almost couldn't stop herself from slashing his tires so he'd have to spend the night.

"See you tomorrow then." She tried to keep her composure.

And that was the night that Myra started flossing. A dentist's wife has to floss every day, she thought. And then she burst into hysterical, ecstatic laughter, not helped by her bloody, beaming smile in the mirror.

ﮐ

Dear Jude,

   I hope you don't have to wait long. I wrote you a poem to
   read when you're bored and lonely and tired of waiting.

   Boxes
   One day you'll be blue,
   instead of just your eyes.
   You'll be locked away,
   and I'll be by your side
   We'll go together, just like we do now.
   Say sayonara to earth and traffic and cubicles.
   Say hello to our next ride.
   Not looking forward to it,
   But thought I'd just say
   That no matter what box you're in—cardboard, mansion,
   coffin—
   It's next to you I'll lay.

All my love,
Nina

I finally got to read Nina's note. The paper was so thin and
aged. I guess not everything is timeless in here. Except for
me. Not even Ruth was timeless as it turned out. I missed
seeing a familiar face. This was the first time I'd been here
and not known a soul. Of course, the new manager was expecting me.

   "I thought Donna was the new manager. Where's

Donna?" I was confused.

"She was the one before me." An older Hispanic man peered at me through horn-rimmed glasses. I thought of an old joke, "He has more chins than a Chinese phone book." And then I felt bad. But I still couldn't stop staring at his massive stomach.

"So she wasn't immortal like Ruth?"

"Don't know what you're talkin' about, kid. Name's Hondie, by the way, not that your ass asked."

I smiled sheepishly and shook his hand. "Sorry." I'd been distracted by the note, which he'd handed to me promptly after I went up to the desk and said, "My name is Jude Floyd. There should be letter for me." I didn't know he was the almighty manager.

"You say immortal?" He was sucking on a toothpick. He must be from around where I'm from, I thought.

"Uh, yeah. Donna didn't tell you about Ruth?"

"Heard of her, that's about it." I didn't know whether to be afraid of this guy or what. I don't think he'd blinked once. Just staring at me real hard.

"Oh. Well she…she was manager for a real long time."

Hondie nodded his head slowly. His chins moved and creased. I realized shortly that he wasn't going to ask any more questions. That was it. That was Hondie. I got used to it eventually. I even came to appreciate it. He never asked my story, although I'm sure Donna had told him all about it. He never asked me anything; he was just fine knowing what he knew and nothing more.

In return, I never asked him why *he* was here. I'd heard enough sad tales anyway.

In the next few days, I met: Rita, the grungy meth addict; Dex, the teenage pill-popper (and dealer); and Sonya, the alcoholic. They called this place "The Recovery Room." They'd even written something in "the addition" about it:

This is a place of healing. This is a place to be the person you wish you still were and hope to be similar to again next time. You can be whoever you want in here. You can see all your past mistakes as well as all the good you've done. You can reflect, you can see more clearly here than you'll ever be able to in life. And maybe one day, those reflections will somehow stick. And you won't make the same mistakes. You'll get a real second chance. Not just a second chance at life, but a second chance to be the best version of yourself.

Not only that, but this new recovering group had invited others to tell their stories. The addition had grown and grown and it was still growing. Random people would relay their journeys to one of the workers, they'd type it up, and publish it! Just like that. I wondered what Ruth would've thought.

I flipped through the stories slowly, eventually reading them all (in between watching Myra and our four children and our nine grandchildren).

You wouldn't believe some of the stuff people had been through. Up until this point, Nina and I had lived all of our lives in the 20th century, as a reasonably "normal" couple. Granted, we were fairly new to this whole life thing.

One story really caught my eye—this guy had been a slave-owning Confederate soldier in his first life and an ex-slave fighting for the Union in his second life. Both lives he'd died in battle. "For all I know, I could've taken a shot at myself…both my selves…at the same damn time." He said after that, he'd been Anglo every time, but never racist. "It doesn't matter that you can't remember your past lives when you're livin' another one. That kind of experience—bein' whipped, watching my daddy hang and my wife sold—that don't leave your soul, never."

I immediately thought: Nina will be ecstatic. Even if this man, whoever he was, was just an exception, one random example…that would be enough for Nina. This would prove to her that people can change and grow and learn. It was enough for me.

I guess this *was* The Recovery Room.

Another makeover of the room was the walls. They were covered with paper—art, poetry, more testimonies—you name it. Everyone was either milling around, looking at it all, or rushing to create something of their own.

"This is all so amazing." I gestured around the room.

"It helps people." Hondie was a lot like Yoda I decided.

Every inch of the boring eggshell was covered. Even some of the "computers" were covered.

"Don't people ever get mad that the papers are blocking their view?" I remembered those first 52 years, when hardly anything could pry me away from watching Nina.

"People spend a lot less time staring out of the windows now," Hondie explained.

"Who's idea was all this?"

"Mine." Of course. He didn't sound cocky, although he had every right to be. Then I noticed his hands—every finger was smudged black. I walked back over to a sketch that stood out from all the rest. It was beautiful and intricate and smoky. It was of a woman laughing. At the bottom, a tiny "Alejandro." I walked around the room, keeping my eye out for pastel sketches in all black. They were all his and they were all the best I'd ever seen.

I should've known—who else has the time to create such masterpieces in this place? Don't get me wrong, other works were really great (especially for taking under an hour to complete), but Hondie's were...unbelievable.

"Have you ever wondered if you're Picasso or Monet or Da Vinci? Reincarnated?" I asked him one day, 100 percent serious.

He chuckled slowly, twirling the toothpick in his mouth. "I don't waste time wondering when I could be sketching."

"So who's the hottie?" I pointed to one of her dancing. She was pictured quite a few times.

"Ex-wife." He coughed and started drawing something on a napkin. I didn't ask any more questions for a while.

If only this would've been here on my first tour of duty, I thought. I could spend all day reading the stories, looking at the art...it was practically a museum. And the best part was, it changed every day.

There was one story about a woman who'd been a man in her first life and first life only. "I was born in Paris in

1692 and from the day I could piece together a single feeling, I knew I wanted to be a woman. I was meant to be a woman. And that's what I've been ever since. Twelve lives and counting. It's like this place was built for corrections."

I liked that a lot. Corrections. And there was so much that needed to be corrected.

"So you're kind of like an addict talent agent, huh?" I asked Hondie after a few months of living in "The Showcase," as I sometimes fondly called it.

"Eh?" You don't expect a man of such few words (not that "eh" is really a word) to be such an artistic genius. Not to mention his size. He looked more like a fullback...who ate a halfback.

"Well Rita plays piano, Dex is a sculptor, and Sonya's a singer. And they're all much better than 'good' or 'great'. There has to be a connection here. I mean, you chose them right?"

Rita had brought a small keyboard in one day and played for me. Pretty sure my jaw hit the floor. Dex followed suit and brought in all his equipment and in the next month, created a goddess that put Michelangelo to shame (then again, I couldn't help thinking that he probably *was* Michelangelo). And Sonya. Sonya didn't need anything. Whether she was at the desk, nonchalantly humming or in front of the entire room belting Whitney Houston to loud cheers and applause, her voice was stunning. I'd never heard such raw talent. She wasn't even trying, it seemed.

"Yeah, I chose them." He *was* manager after all.

"Do you have some kind of plot to make the world

notice them or something?" He gave me another one of his slow chuckles. "How can the world *not* notice them?"

"All I care about is the fact that none of 'em have used in over a year. They'll probably be outta this safe house pretty soon."

"But they've barely been here!"

His chins jiggled more. "I'm not their daddy. I'm not gonna coddle 'em for the rest of their lives. Others need a chance to recover. It's not a place to be selfish."

I thought on that one for a while. Was Nina's and my whole set-up considered selfish? I'd read in the handbook and all over the walls about other loves, loves that seemed so comparable to ours. Why weren't they given a chance?

Looking around the room, I remembered when this place used to be bare and clean and boring and quiet. Ruth's rules of no music and no nothing really. Just waiting. But now? It was so much more than waiting. And it was the opposite of bare, clean, boring, and quiet. Newspaper covered an entire corner of the room, and bits of Dex's clay mixture covered the newspaper. A mock-stage was in another corner, with Rita's keyboard and a mic and stand for Sonya. Chairs were stacked high with art supplies, writing supplies, music sheets, and more. Honestly, it looked like a preschool of prodigies had exploded in here.

Would any of this have happened without Nina and "the addition"? Did we start some kind of creative disease that just kept on growing and growing and growing? It's funny to think what or who has the power to change the world. Granted, this is the world of "in between". I won't say this is the world of death, but it certainly isn't the world of life. The same concept applies though—one moment, one reunited couple, can have a bigger impact than I ever thought possible.

꿍

Just like Hondie had said, replacements weren't far behind. New recovering "talents" came in, red-eyed and shaky. A novelist, a guitarist, a ballerina. I thought of the time Nina had sighed and said, "All the greats were druggies or alcoholics. That's probably why I haven't been published yet. I'm not messed up enough. I haven't overdosed." I'd waved off her statement then, but now I wondered if it had some truth to it…

Then there was a drummer, an opera singer, a Broadway star. After that? A poet, a painter, and a rapper. The last round before Nina arrived was a comedian, a yodeler (yes, really, a yodeler), and a cellist.

I told Hondie that thanks to him, I was officially becoming "cultured". I'd never heard him laugh for so long. His toothpick almost fell out of his mouth.

"The Showcase," "The Waiting Room," "The Recovery Room," whatever you want to call it—it literally began holding galleries and performances almost daily. I felt like a character in a book, living inside some quasi-museum-amphitheater. All we needed was cheese and wine. I felt like I was constantly surrounded by the most talented people in the world. And then I realized that I probably always had been…they just weren't encouraged to show off before.

Now instead of moping, people were having sing-offs, dance-offs, duets. They were getting tips from other artists, sharing experiences, drawing portraits of each other. Or they were just taking it all in, watching the beauty around them, reading as many testimonies as they could.

A lot of times, it was hard to get people out of the door on time. They were having too much fun. They were learning too much. Being dead. Isn't that absolutely, positively ridiculous? I loved every minute of it.

And so did Nina when she got there. It was six years after I'd died. I'd hardly spent any time at all watching her, but I knew she wouldn't care. She probably preferred it that way.

This was the first time we didn't make love in the break room. I didn't want to take up any of her time. I'd had six whole years of this and she only had six hours!

"It's so...it's so..." She was flabbergasted. She even hugged Hondie, which made him blush and get this confused look on his face. I laughed my ass off and then he crinkled his eyebrows and tried to look stern and manly and unaffected. But that just led to shy chuckles and chin jiggling.

Nina cried, walking around and around the room. She suddenly ran up to me, clutching a paper in her hand. "Do you realize that no one says anything like 'All my lives have been shit!'?' No one complains that they haven't had some sort of redemption. Everyone has had at least one great, happy life. Read this."

The handwriting was sloppy and cursive.

I've been addicted to just about everything evil on this planet. Heroin, crack, meth, vodka, cigarettes, abusive relationships…you name it. My lives seemed to get worse and worse every time. I've died young, I've accidentally overdosed three times, I've died in an alley, I've been homeless too many times to count. I've sold my body to anyone with a buck. I've sold my soul to the devil. And my last life probably would've been more of the same. But something happened. I met someone and he saved me before I could even think about doing something that I would need saving from. I lived a normal, simple, boring life in a real house with a real family and a real job. I was a wife and a mother and that was all—nothing too special according to most people. But it was the best life I've ever lived and all I ever want is to keep living ones just like it. And I'm sure now that he's found me once, he'll find me and save me again and forever.

"This has to mean something, right?" she asked, when she saw I was done reading.

"Yeah," I agreed, "but what exactly?" It was a great, touching story but…did it really mean anything? For all we knew, her next life after writing that could've been the worst one yet.

"I just feel like this place is so much more important than anyone realizes. Obviously our thoughts and decisions in here affect our next life." I had never seen her so struck by passion. And I didn't want to bring her down but…

"What do you think happened in here that made her next life change so drastically from all the rest?" I mean, it's a good point. What can you really accomplish in an hour, half an hour, a few minutes?

"You don't think that seeing all of this," she spun around like a little kid, waving her arms at the walls, "could change a person? Just suddenly hitting them like a bag of bricks?"

"I guess that's pretty hard to say." I shrugged, unconvinced, just like I was still unconvinced on the Christianity train she'd jumped on.

"Think about it logically. We can never stop learning and growing as individuals, right?"

"Sure." I gave her a quick kiss on the cheek before she could swat me away.

"So it's not like we can ever have a 100 percent perfect life. I mean, I guess we could; it's all about perspective, but I'm just saying, there's always room for development. Of any kind. If you're open to it. In here." She was breathing hard. It reminded me of the time she ranted about how rich we'd be if we opened a Hooters-equivalent restaurant named Bananas.

I tried to hide my smile. "Well, my love, I agree with you that this place is our sanctuary, our holy grail. But only because it brought you back to me." I shrugged and she sighed, obviously disappointed in my lack of zeal.

"I guess that's good enough for now." She leaned into me and we walked around the room together, listening to the cellist until it was time.

ﮌ

Alex & Josh

"I'm like red wine and Cheerio's," he'd said, popping a chili cheese fry in his mouth.

We were 22, and it was our third summer reuniting between semesters of my business classes and his...well, whatever his job was this week. We had agreed the day he helped me box up my sock drawer that we weren't going to be one of those disgusting "long distance couples." We shared strong hatreds: meatloaf, babies, our middle names, driving the speed limit, and long distance couples. We weren't even really ever "together" anyway, so it wasn't a big deal. Why make things harder?

He hated our town so much that he'd talked about moving with me, waiting tables. But he couldn't afford to move out of his mom's place. We'd never said those three words, never talked about "our future"—we were just never into that whole show and tell act. I mean, for God's sake, I knew everything about him. I used to cover the burns his dad left on his arms with my make up in middle school. He knew every single one of my pet peeves, fears, dreams. He used to say that he'd counted and memorized my freckles throughout the years. I never told him that I'd done the same with his.

"You say the weirdest shit." We were a little tipsy, even though it was three in the afternoon. We met at Brookeville's only bar. He'd been waiting for me all day, but I had to make the yearly family visit.

"No, think about it. Red wine and Cheerio's."

"Nope. Got nothin'."

"I'm good for your heart, Al!"

I try not to think about what happened after that. He kind of fumbled down to the peanut shell-covered floor and pulled out a tiny box with a tiny ring inside.

"Alex Maureen Reister, you know I'm a fuck up. Everybody knows that. But the only thing that keeps me sane is seeing you every once in awhile. I'm tired of being so far away, pretending to have a life. You *are* my life." He shrugged sheepishly, cheeks pink, beer caught in his unshaven beard. "Marry me?"

I'd said no. I loved him more than anything I could think of.

I grew up in one of those places that screamed consistently with train whistles. It helped me sleep at night. He literally came from the other side of the tracks, which we always joked about. Sipping on Sonic sweet tea in the abandoned Deaf Learning Center was our favorite. It'd been shut down since I was in elementary school, but whoever owned it never sold the land or anything. It was nice, too. Big, stretching glass windows and fancy metal door handles. Never locked either. We'd tiptoe inside like we were breaking into a museum. But other kids had decorated the walls and scuffed the tile. We liked the huge bench outside the back entrance.

"I wish we were deaf sometimes," he'd said one day. It was one of the first times I remembered him touching me. It was his pointer finger on my shoulder I concluded later, even though he'd been sitting behind me so who really knows.

"Jesus Christ Josh, why?"

"Well not only would I be saved from these trains, but think about it. Me and you, we'd open this place up, we'd never have to deal with people's bullshit..." His voice trailed off and he shook around the leftover ice in his cup. He'd moved to Brookeville when he was eight, which I thought was plenty of time to treat the trains like lullabies, but apparently not.

"I never really knew why they closed it down. But c'mon, how many deaf people do you know anywhere around us?" My left shoulder blade was still tingling.

"Now that I think about it, why'd we have to be deaf to open it? We should do it Al, I'm serious."

"All you practically know is the freakin' alphabet in sign language. You just don't want to think about graduating."

"Forget it." And just like that, I'd pissed him off again.

I always made straight A's; it seemed to be the only thing I was good at. In fifth grade, Josh taught me how to skate and draw and climb a tree. I did his homework up to sophomore year. He smoked and drank and rode his bike around town instead of going to math. So it wasn't a big surprise that he wasn't applying to college. Didn't suit him really. But I'd been wearing my dad's alma mater colors since I was born and it just made sense. Thing was, I'd be ten hours away from home, ten hours away from him.

"I'm sorry, but it's true. It's not like we'll never see each other. Jesus Christ you're my best friend."

He touched a little more than my shoulder then,

scooting up to sit beside me, grasping my clammy neck with both his clammy hands.

"You're my best friend too," he'd whispered in between kisses.

And that was our summer. He was my first everything, and that's how I'd always wanted it. Everyone always thought I never had boyfriends because I was just "one of those girls," too focused on grades with no time for anything else. And Josh got away with being alone because…he was Josh. No one ever talked to him because he refused to let them. He preferred being alone. "No one but you really understands me," he used to say. I could never shake the feeling that he latched on to me because he knew I'd always be there, not because he loved me. I never understood him. But I think I'd always been waiting for him to try desperately to unhook my bra in the learning center lobby.

I was almost 33 when I bought it. Most of what we did was train interpreters and teach children and their family members. Fifty years ago, the school would've been packed—people couldn't imagine deaf people attending "regular" schools. Now I understood why the wrinkled faded man I'd met with had closed it down.

"I've been waiting for you," he'd said with a wheezy chuckle. "I knew someday someone would see the potential in my little bungalow." He had refused to sell the building to anyone who wanted to open a mall or a restaurant or anything besides his dream. Both his parents were deaf and he said he'd never forget the look of pride in their faces when they saw him mouth sounds they'd never hear. I envied his happiness, his memories, his success; I envied the pictures on his desk of young smiles.

I had money by then—I think I started saving the day Josh stumbled out of the bar that day. Fresh paint, teachers, fancy equipment—none of it seemed out of reach, and I took my time. I wanted to get it just right. I knew he was waiting.

I didn't do much, though. I was mainly known as "that crazy rich woman on a mission," but I began sitting in on classes. I found myself mesmerized. I had always been about numbers—how boring. My old boring, number-filled executive job paid for a world I became lost in. Stories, explanations, questions, fights—all with flicks of knuckles and jerks of wrists. I could never even read *myself*. Now I was surrounded by people who took one swift glance at my eyes and *knew*. They just *knew*. They'd all had a lifetime of turning others into books and there I was, illiterate.

It took me three weeks to work up the nerve to call him, even though I'd rehearsed the conversation in my head for a decade. Four rings and he finally picked up. It had taken me forever to track down his new number. He'd moved to Oregon, of all places.

"Yel-lo." *So he still said that.* I smiled.

"Look, please don't say anything till I'm done. Please don't hang up, Josh." I sounded so rushed, like the world was on a ticking time bomb. "I think about you every day. I've thought about you every day since you called me four-eyes in second grade and I've thought about you every day since you proposed. And I bought it, Josh. I bought our center and I have everything ready—teachers, students." I was smiling thinking of little Jaime, knowing he'd adore her. "There's this one little angel and she's five and she's teaching me more than I'm teaching her and I love it. Today she taught me the word *cookie*; you should see her tiny fingers. And she's already improved on lip reading. It'll be just like you always talked about. I'll even buy every train in the damn state if that helps; shut 'em all down. I never want to go another day without your voice and I guess what I'm trying to say is that I'm red wine and Cheerio's. I'm red wine and Cheerio's." I laughed.

Silence.

You know when you create a victory, a happy ending? You build it up in your head for so long that your cheeks and your stomach and your throat tighten with pure happiness—before anything really happens. I wavered for a second, thinking *it's all over*. He must have a girlfriend or wife or kids… I could feel his chest and arms and hug over the phone.

"Josh?"

I thought of when I learned how to sign *I love you* and *sex* and *marriage*. My manicured hands were slow in comparison to everyone else.

World and *life* and *lips* and *chicken fried steak*, his favorite.

He had taught me all the bad words. I remembered his thumb folding into his palm to make a *B*. He jutted the letter away from his chin when he was mad at me. *Bitch*.

My hands related him to everything. *Princess* and *prince*, *girlfriend*, *wife*, *best friend*.

131

"I'm here," he whispered. "But I'll be back to you soon."
Forever.

ॐ

"What the fuck is wrong with you?" He hardly ever used that word to her, especially right in her face. It was like a slap. But what was she thinking, bringing up something like that? He felt like he'd never been this mad or hurt—in all their lives together, this just had to be the place where they got in their most tumultuous fight. *How ironic*, he thought.

"No, Jude, what the fuck is wrong with *you*? Obviously, I was just trying to start a philosophical discussion. But no, of course, you can't talk about anything without getting butt hurt like a child."

"A philosophical discussion about which one of us has screwed up the most? Is that supposed to be light-hearted and casual? Or is the real kicker the part where you clearly think I'm the fuck-up and you're perfect?" He was yelling now, red in the face, inches away from hers. Everyone in The Waiting Room could hear them through the break room wall. The infamous Jude and Nina were fighting? This was unbelievable to everyone else—this couple was supposed to be "The Chosen Ones," the epitome of a successful marriage. They were supposed to show everyone else how it was done. They were supposed to somehow change the world, put everything after death in some kind of magical order, allowing everyone to wait on whomever they wanted to.

Listening to them fight was like the paparazzi catching the big break of their career on film. Many people in the room, including the loud and boisterous new manager, thought *Well, this is it. Their reign of waiting is over. Mission failed.*

"I didn't ask which one of us had screwed up the most! I was just talking about some of the decisions we've made and how they affected our lives and how they're maybe affecting our future lives!"

"No, Nina, you weren't talking about *our* decisions, you were talking specifically about *mine*. About how I let you move to New York by yourself and I took a few years to follow you. About how I ran away after you refused to marry me. About how I've never been anything close to a big shot like you have. Sorry I've never been extremely rich or extremely talented or extremely intelligent! Is that what this is about?"

"No, of course-"

"Because I hate to break it to you, but you've fallen in love with me every single time. So if you're so dissatisfied, then why don't you just stay the fuck away from me next time?"

"Jude, I-"

"No, you know what? Why don't we go ahead and try that out? When our names come up, I don't want to walk through with you. Who knows, maybe this whole time, that's the reason we keep getting together. Because you obviously don't think enough of me to *want* to be with me on your own. It's obviously just some sort of fluke by this stupid room. So sorry to be such a burden and obligation on you." He swung open the door fiercely and walked out into a room full of people who quickly looked away or pretended to be in conversation with the person next to them.

The manager handed him a sheet of paper, nervously looking the opposite direction and tapping her feet on the floor. It was time. Nina was just walking out of the break room, wiping her eyes and smoothing her hair self-consciously. She'd told Jude once, "We have to act like a presidential couple or something. Everybody looks to us to set some sort of example." He'd jokingly walked around the room with her, arm in arm, waving pompously with a fixed fake smile and a puffed out chest.

Jude looked from her to the paper, still shaking with near-rage. And then he ran through the door without looking back, letting the single sheet with their names printed on it neatly fall to the ground.

Gasps filled the room. Nina screamed his name, even though he was gone. She almost fell running after him, leaping through the doorway frantically.

CHAPTER 6

Jennifer & Eric

It was the first time I decided to brave the waters and take Eric to meet my family. Thanksgiving and a jalapeño turkey. It was Uncle Ray's idea, of course, and it seemed like everyone was thoroughly excited about the "spicy white meat and the spicier dark meat" except me. Why not make jalapeño cornbread? That's semi-normal. Or crackers with that jalapeño cream cheese. I guess they couldn't think of anything that really said "Thank you pilgrims and Native Americans" more than the green-speckled bird in front of me. So I was left aimlessly trying to dilute the zestiness of the meat with mashed potatoes and green bean casserole. My cousin Cayden looked at me from across the table and rolled his eyes as he took a large bite of fruit salad.

"Excuse me, no one's said grace yet." My Aunt Denise eyed Cayden's mouthful.

She stopped making him spit it out a few years ago, but I miss the ridicule I could afterwards use to my advantage. Cayden swallowed and grinned at me as his mother began her usual speech.

"Thank You Heavenly Father for this gift we've received (*the burn our throats will soon face?*). We are so lucky to be sitting here in this house, surrounded by our loved ones. This year marks a new era for us, as You know. My dear sister has passed, but we know You're taking wonderful care of her."

I knew this would turn ugly. It usually does when you mix my family with large amounts of food and dim lights. My cheeks flushed with anger as I tried to breathe like my 7th grade P.E. coach had taught us. *Inhale quickly twice through your nose, exhale once through your mouth. Inhale quickly twice through your nose, exhale once through your mouth.* Of course, that was for running a mile in numbered gray outfits, not constraining yourself from leaping across a table with a butter knife, but it was worth a shot. I closed my eyes a little too tightly, pretending to be immersed in prayer. Well, I was praying, technically. That by the end of this dinner, Eric wouldn't run out of my life as quickly as he'd run into it. We were 22 and I had given up on men entirely. College was full of douchebags trying to get into my pants. But then I met Eric. So I wasn't pretending to pray, I was just pretending to pray about my Aunt Isabelle.

The thing was, no one ever mentioned Uncle Milt. Yeah, Aunt Isabelle was "blood," but she'd been married to Uncle Milt for over 30 years! What kind of family didn't accept a 30-year in-law? Who even says in-law anymore? The lovely speech continued.

"We hope she's watching down upon us today and

always, with her beautiful green eyes (*green like the fifties she used to slip in everyone's hands after dessert*). Amen."

It was over? Yup, tear-stained faces in every direction, small coughs and sobs coming from high collared shirts and pearled necks.

Cayden's guest (*why would you ever bring an innocent by-stander to a holiday? Oh, that's right, I was making the same mistake.*) was staring at his glass of water as if at any moment he would dive in and escape this train wreck like a cube of ice. Oh, and when I say guest, I mean boyfriend, but we don't want anyone getting shot, now do we? I'll never forget that Christmas when a tall, blonde, awkward teenager was announced by Uncle Ray as "Cayden's best friend, Justin. They play sports together." No one ever cared enough to ask what sport either of them played. If they would have, Cayden might've said, "Um…rugby?" looked at his dad, and then said, "Yeah, rugby." And Justin would've answered honestly with a simple, "I play the clarinet."

"Uh…nice to meet all of you, I've heard a lot about you," the poor boy had stammered. I shook my head, thinking, *doesn't Cayden know not to bring anyone here unless it's the person he's going to marry?*

"Of course you've heard about us, son. Because you two are best buddies from school." Uncle Ray had laughed too loud and too short and clapped a giant hand on Justin's back.

It amazed me how Cayden was now 21 years old and not one family member realized that almost every year since his 17th birthday, a different male acquaintance was introduced to us as a "lab partner" or "fellow employee of American Eagle." The latest was "Tristan, his fraternity brother." This was a bit over the top, but I'd had fun with it during Easter.

"So did you guys get hazed much? I hear they tie you up and blindfold you and make you swallow things." I had smiled innocently over the pastel centerpiece of bunnies and flowers. Tristan's ears turned hot pink and Cayden pretended to choke on his honey-baked ham.

Now, as my mother was dabbing at her mascara beside me, Tristan looked ready to say that the Kappa Alpha's had a mandatory meeting in five minutes. Cayden flared his nostrils in embarrassment and I slyly texted him under the table.

"I can't see either of ur hands. Not appropriate."

I watched his shoulders relax as he read it and tried to contain his laughter. Everyone began eating and my anger pressured my lips into opening. This was bullshit. *Please still love me after this*, I said in my head, squeezing Eric's knee.

"I think we forgot to mention someone in that beautiful grace, Aunt Denise." I glanced from face to face, trying to see anything besides stuffing crumbs lining the corners of mouths.

"Who, dear?" My grandma looked genuinely concerned, as if perhaps Paul McCartney died and no one had told her.

"Oh, I don't know, maybe the other mem-ber of our fam-i-ly who was also on that plane?" I felt like grabbing old pictures, circling Uncle Milt's head, and passing the photos around the table, but then I remembered that they always asked him to be the cameraman.

"Please do not speak to your grandmother that way." My dad said to his spoon of cranberry sauce.

"I'm speaking to the whole table actually. My uncle who collected stamps and wore cartoon ties is dead." It was me who was crying now, remembering the smell of dusty books and cheap cologne when I hugged him. "My uncle who never tried to buy my love, my uncle who told me horrible jokes and taught me the roman numerals when all the other men were smoking cigars. That is who I hope is watching over me, not the alcoholic millionaire who brought her first husband as a date to Aunt Rachel's second wedding."

The room stared at me as if I'd just told them they'd have to live in only single-story houses from now on. Uncle Ray started buttering his roll.

"Well, Amen." I stood up, tossing my napkin down on my jalapeño catastrophe.

"I want come!" Two-year old Davey reached his palms up out of his highchair.

"Maybe next year, sweetie. Cayden, if you and your boyfriend would like to come, that's fine. Although I must say, I think he's a little too short for you, no offense, Tristan."

"None taken."

"He's my fraternity brother..." Cayden whispered, sinking down an inch in his seat.

"I wasn't aware that there were gay frats, but what a novel idea. Are the kegs filled with flirtinis?"

I glared at him and he glared back. And then we both

burst into laughter. I stormed out of the dining room with two giggling men (plus Eric) behind me.

"I was thinkin' IHOP, but if you guys would prefer Denny's, that's cool too."

Eric, always a gentleman, bowed a little when he got up from the table and said, "So nice to meet all of you." And then when we were almost to the $3,000 oak doors that had been installed last week: "Oh and I hope I have your blessing because I want to marry that woman."

When he appeared, his stomach was in knots. What if he'd fucked everything up? What if Jennifer wasn't Nina at all? And now he'd be here an hour or so and then get called, alone, and that's how it would be forever. He dropped his head in his hands and sobbed, finally moving aside a sketch of someone's dog to look out and watch Jennifer. She had to be Nina. He just knew it. Just like he'd felt it all the other times.

He tried to control his breathing, literally holding down his right fist to stop it from punching the window. Why did he run out the door? Why was he so stupid?

After half a day, he was confident that he was waiting. But still—what if this gorgeous woman and mother to his children that he'd been watching for seven hours straight—what if she wasn't Nina? Did that mean now he was waiting for her, this mystery woman? Or would he still be waiting for Nina, even though she spent her life with who knows who doing who knows what. Surely they couldn't just skip a life together and then just go back to the way things were. Jude stressed over this every minute of every day. He hardly ate or even spoke. The employees would whisper to each other, and he sometimes heard bits and pieces.

"This isn't what I heard he was like."

"I'm too scared to even ask him what's wrong."

"He looks crazy."

"He won't even tell me how old he was when he died. Then maybe we'd know how much longer he'll be here."

"What if he messed up so bad that now he's going to be here forever?"

That idea worried him the most. He hadn't even thought of that. It'd be the perfect punishment. Therefore, Nina could've already died and been sent along to her next life for all he knew. And he'd just be stuck here, not knowing, not even rotting.

God, I wish I could rot, he thought every single day. Until Nina showed up, of course.

Allysia & George

Rain formed sketchy rivers on the windshield of Mom's Honda Pilot and I lounged in the passenger seat, waiting for her to finish buying who knows what in HEB. I stopped going into grocery stores with her ages ago. She's nuts about groceries. She'll never buy off-brand anything! One time, I picked up some cream cheese-cream cheese! And she made me return it because I bought the Wal-Mart brand, the dollar less kind. I mean, how different could they be? But that's not the real reason that I stopped going into grocery stores with her. Have you ever been just walking down the cereal aisle with your mom and she's ranting on and on about your clothes, your weight, your makeup, your hair, your attitude, or your future—and you realize that you don't ever want to go anywhere with this woman again? Well I don't know when exactly it hit me, but probably around the millionth time that I heard, "Allysia, for God's sake, spit out your gum *before* we walk into stores. It looks so ugly." I got tired of spitting out my gum before the flavor faded.

I slid off my brown flip-flops, propping my feet on the dash, and changed the radio station with my big toe. *What an exciting Saturday*. The lady next to my window had a pile of at least six loaves of bread in her cart and I stared at them being loaded into her trunk one by one. My head hurt. Not from the bread or the rain, but from the divorce. It's not exactly easy to grow up cheery and optimistic *and* a kid of divorce. Hasn't like 99% of the country gone through this though? So why are there any happy people left? Maybe they're faking. These days you're either a divorcee or a divorcee relative. I am the latter only because I'm not old enough to get married. But when I do, I'm positive that I'll divorce at least three times. What the hell, gotta heighten those statistics. The first time, he can get into drugs and start hitting me. The second guy will cheat on me and spend all his time at work. I'll absolutely adore the third guy; he'll be a complete saint. But I'll be confused and divorce him just the same. This is the way I think. Well, thought. Before I met George.

I sighed loud enough for the bread lady to turn around and give me a strange look. Not really, but I imagined sighing that loudly, and it made me smile. This is what happens when you listen to slow songs alone in the rain in a parking lot. You get a kick out of sighing.

Divorce is simply a catalyst for bitter, cynical, sarcastic people. And I'm not mad to be a part of this group. I like this group. I love half-empty glasses. So I'm not mad at who I am, I'm mad at why I am the way I am. Which doesn't make any sense when you think about it, because if I like myself, why should I hate the influences that have turned me into who I am? That's just the way it goes I guess. I don't like myself as much as I let on. Not that I'm some cocky bastard, I'm just confident. But I don't know, if I had the choice to become a thrilled-to-be-alive pious motivational speaker or something, would I take it? Yeah, you're right, probably not.

I hate the child support that we've never received and I hate the whole half of my family that I lost and couldn't care less about. I hate tight-lipped conversations about "your father" and I hate it when she cries. See, the thing is, my parents got divorced years ago. The last time I even saw my biological sperm bank was a decade ago. And while a handful of my friends are going through horrible divorces *right now*, I'm sitting here in front of Blockbuster thinking about my good for nothing father that sent me a letter from rehab yesterday. It was written in rehab format. I'm familiar with this vomit-inducing arrangement of words from past letters and Lifetime movies. His obvious forced penmanship gleams off the paper, daring me to rip it into shreds. The fake sincerity, the way he calls me "Aly baby," or his forever signature of "Love, Daddy." Something keeps me reading, but nothing keeps me writing. That's the only reason I'm sitting in this Pilot right now. Mom feels she needs me to conquer the apparently frightening produce section—she never wants to go alone. But as she took her keys out of the ignition, I said innocently, "I think I'm going to write my father back." She was suddenly eager to get every item scratched off her list as slowly as possible. I have a pen. I have paper. I even have stamps. But what the fuck am I supposed to say? *Hey, thanks for the awesome childhood. Oh wait…that wasn't you.*

As the bread lady pulled out, a gleaming Cadillac pulled in next to me, and it took about 30 minutes for an extremely old couple to slide off of the leather interior. They locked wrinkly hands and smiled nonstop with their pearly dentures. *Don't let them fool you, they've only been married for a month I bet.* Definite divorcees. I glanced over into the Cadillac and spotted something that made me shake my head. Who carries a Bible in their car? *Well, they do obviously, Allysia.* I'm so incredibly anti-religion that it scares me sometimes. And not to blame it on divorce, but I think it's because my parents got divorced. Mom's exact words whenever the topic of religion comes up are as follows: "You know, that's what I regret most. We didn't raise you right. And now you have a bad attitude towards religion. It's so sad." A bad attitude. That makes me giggle. The other day, my friend was talking about our Baccalaureate service (religious graduation "God be with you while you go party in college" thing), and she was like "C'mon Allysia, you need a little Jesus in your life." She knows that I'm the last person to take that advice, and she smiled over her glass of water. Despite frequent attempts to turn me Mormon, she's never succeeded. My mom looked over at me and narrowed her criticizing eyes. The hellish look meant, "don't make a Dane Cook joke," but there was no way I was going to attend some "non-denominational" church party. "I think Jesus needs a little Allysia in his life," I promptly replied, strutting away laughing. Wait, do you capitalize "His" when you're talking about Jesus? Or is that just for the big man? Wow, I'm bad at this. I swiveled the pen in my hand.

Dear Roger,

There. That was enough for now. If he was expecting "Daddy," he could forget it.

The wrinkly couple was just getting to the doors of HEB when a massive minivan pulled up on my left. I'm talking one of those vans you only see in the Tide commercials with the typical soccer mom driving around ten grass-stained boys. Sure enough, there was that mom. That worn-out mom with no make-up, messy hair, old clothes, and sleepy eyes. That mom bringing her three kids to the store and that mom without an accompanying husband. *He probably left them. Or he's watching TV at home. Or he's working. Or cheating on her.* I'm just kidding on that last one, I'm sure he's very loyal. But I'm even more sure that they're divorced. The kids piled out of the van one by one, splashing each other in puddles. The rain had finally stopped, but everything was still so gray. I tried to look at the mom's left hand without leaning out of my seat, but she was trying to catch up with her hooligans. Probably nothing to see on that finger anyway. Except maybe a suntan line. Or worse, a ring that doesn't mean anything anymore.

"Joy to the World" started mixing annoyingly with the radio as my cell phone went off. My big toe tapped the off button and I checked the caller ID. Just Dad.

"What up Daddy-O?"

"Uh. Tell your mom that I need Worcestershire sauce."

"Call her cell phone."

"She doesn't answer it."

"Well she's in HEB already."

"Well go get her."

"How am I supposed to find her, genius?"

"*Allysia*. Go. Now."

"Ughhhhh." *Click*.

I think he can do without steak sauce. I leaned back deeper in the passenger seat. *I couldn't find her*, I practiced. Stepdads. Such a love-hate relationship. He's cool. I mean, he's great. I *have* had him around for years and years, so it's not like he's some weird evil mom-stealer, even though that's what I thought when I was seven. But still, it's pretty competitive if that makes sense. Sometimes, when I'm mad at him, I always seem to imagine him cheating on Mom. In the back of my head, something pushes these thoughts further into reality and I find myself expecting him to mess up, for them to split up. What's one more divorce? He's frustrating, he's stubborn, he's hilarious, he's lazy, and he's good to Mom...but then again, I don't think anyone is good enough for her. She drives me absolutely insane and she annoys me so much that I have to make excuses not to shop for milk and eggs with her. She tells me not to sing in restaurants or dance in public or ever walk out of the house without earrings in. Yet, somehow I love the psycho dyed-blonde more than life itself.

Suddenly, my depressing thoughts were rudely interrupted by a sharp, impatient rapping on the door. "Unlock the car!" I blinked, put the radio back on her beloved country, and slowly pressed the button. Here we go. *Shit, I didn't write the letter!* I scribbled something down and watched Mom loading her brand-name products into the backseat.

"Uh...Dad called, he wanted some Worcestershire sauce."

"I swear that man is so damn picky. We have A1 but nooo..." Her voice trailed off as she closed the door. I always find it funny when she does that. It proves that she's not truly talking to me, just muttering to herself. She plopped in the driver's seat and started the car. "Did you finish the letter?" Her eyes darted to the folded sheet of paper in my hands.

"Um...yeah."

"Can I read it before I start driving?"

"Oh...uh...it's personal, Mom."

"Allysia, for God's sake, how can it be personal?" She

was even more irritated now than when she went inside HEB. I bet she got one of those carts with the wheel that sticks. That drives her crazy.

"Fine. Here." I handed her the paper and waited with my arms crossed.

"Allysia Marie!" I looked up sheepishly. Her eyes and mouth were wide open. And then she did something that I haven't heard in a long, long time. She snorted.

"Oh my gosh, Mom. You totally just snorted." I pursed my lips together and started giggling. Her laughter started getting louder and we both began rocking back and forth in our seats.

"No I didn't!" Her face was turning red.

"Yes you did!" My face was turning red.

"I just can't believe you wrote that!" We had subsided to chuckles.

"Let's go mail it."

"No ma'am we are not." She gripped the steering wheel and exhaled deeply. I put on my seatbelt. She put on her seatbelt. And we drove away stealing glances at each other, smiling.

Dear Roger,

Go screw yourself.

Sincerely,
Allysia

Mom reread the letter at every red light.

And that was me, pre-George. That was how I was in elementary school (I'm not kidding), all through high school, and the beginning of college.

And then I met George in the library. I was studying; he was on Facebook. There was a line of students waiting to use the computers.

"You know, you could probably do that in your dorm room. All those people are waiting." I was kind of a pretentious kid.

"*You know*," mocking my tone, "I don't live in a dorm, I don't have a computer, and I'm actually researching for my essay on social media."

"Oh. Really?"

"No. I wanted to change my status."

We both laughed and then he proceeded to tell me *why* he needed to update his status: his phone was dead, he lost his charger, and he didn't have enough money to buy another one. So he was letting everyone know via Facebook, including his mom.

Long story short, we had the same phone. Two of the only people left on the planet who still had flip phones. So we worked out a schedule for him to come over and charge his phone every day...which led to a relationship of course. The last thing I wanted.

That was the same semester I met Jacobo.

It wasn't so much intrigue. That's just a movie-word. "She was intrigued by him." No. It was just...well, it was just that he was a goddamn poet. He spoke Spanish and he had a really strange name and he wrote these poems...you just can't understand until you read them. They're fucking long too. But I soaked up every word like a schoolgirl crushing on her English teacher. I wasn't allowed to have crushes though. I had a boyfriend, an amazing one at that. So I just read the poems and listened to his words and watched his forearm expectantly.

He had a tattoo of a bird in a birdcage. I wanted to know if he had a bird. You never know. Or if he was the bird. And in that case, who was the cage? What was the cage?

He got up in front of the whole class and said, "The body is just a shell used to carry around our souls."

Why did he say shell and not cage? His lips philoso-phized Christine de Pizan while he wore a Popeye t-shirt. And yet, everyday I checked the arm, the shell, to see if the bird had escaped.

Of course, in true cliché form, he was scheduled to do his research essay on the same book as me. A book of let-ters between a man and a woman.

"So how are we gonna do this?" His jet-black hair sang tenor against his pale skin.

"Well I haven't even started reading." He laughed.

"Me either," I lied. "I guess just email me or something?"

"Do you have Facebook?" Oh lord. He had dimples and he'd find me and see my profile picture, which was of me and my dimpled-boyfriend.

"Yeah. My name is spelled weird though. A-L-L-Y-S-I-A. Yeah, I'll just find you."

"What's your last name?" He was one of those calm peo-ple, great.

"Aguilar. Yours?"

"Aguirre."

"Ah, should be easy then, they're so similar." Was I trying to make a joke? Not sure, but he graciously grinned.

"Ok then, cool." And he walked away. Found me by the end of that night. Guess I'm not as mysterious as I'd like to think.

So the book. How fitting, right? Not to mention, my presentation turned out to be focused on one of Heloise's letters while his on one of Abelard's. Not that I'm comparing us to them. I'm in no way a nun and I hope he hasn't been castrated. Not to say that I want to use his non-castrated penis in any way, shape, or form. I'm just saying, I hope, for *his* sake, that he's still, well, together.

It was the second day of class that I really wanted to know more. See? Curiosity, not intrigue. Besides, he was too short for me.

"It's Huck, like Huck Finn, and then Obo, like the instrument. Jacobo."

Took our teacher weeks to figure that one out. But I ate it up. People always call me Ashley.

The day our essays were due, I smiled over my shoulder and whispered, "How'd yours turn out?"

He shrugged. "I skimmed, but we'll see I guess."

That was a little disappointing, but I thought maybe he was being modest. His presentation was great, after all. I'm sure his palms weren't as clammy as mine. And besides, it's impossible to *not* find Heloise fascinating. Surely he saw the beauty of questioning the church during that time (and pre-marital intercourse with your teacher).

But when our frizzy-haired feminist professor handed

back our papers, mine bore a small A- while the birdcage tried to hide a large D. I suddenly noticed flecks of dried up hair gel lining his brow. I never asked about his tattoo, but the black ink was probably just a representation of a band's CD art.

George and I celebrated the fact that we weren't members of the monastery three times that night. And not just that for-the-hell-of-it sex. It was that sweat-through-your-bra, bite-the-corner-of-the-pillow sex. He thought I was in a good mood because of my grade. And I guess it was, in part. I'd worked all week on that six-page masterpiece.

But the truth is, sometimes you just fall in love with guys named George who speak English and Pig Latin and neither very well. Guys who actually enjoy church, hate poetry, never have their names mispronounced, and don't pretend to care about a class if they really just don't give a shit.

Until he fell asleep, my fingers swam across George's gel-free head and bare, flawless arm. I never thought about my future divorces after that.

Nina was playing Checkers with a six-year old named Ariel. It was like a Christmas present. There were never children in The Waiting Room. Mainly because, well, no one's best life was when they died before puberty. But Ariel was new, her very first life cut short. She was pig-tailed and doe-eyed and Nina loved feeling like a mother again, even if it was just for an hour or so.

"Have you ever seen The Little Mermaid?" she asked, letting Ariel take a sip from her water bottle.

"No." She gave Nina a confused look, scrunching up her tiny, peach fuzz eyebrows.

Nina held in a laugh. *Of course she'd never heard of it, Ariel was probably from an age where Disney movies don't even exist.* That idea made her hold in another laugh. Who knows when or where she was from. Nina was, in a way, too scared to ask. She didn't want to know what the future was like. It's funny how no one ever has high hopes for the future, as far as humanity is concerned. Sure, they're excited about the medicines and technologies. But the way people have changed over the years? Nina thought that sometimes, it's unclear whether we're taking steps forward or backward. She hoped and prayed that The Waiting Room was somehow changing that, somehow making the future a better place. But she was too scared to ever ask anyone.

Ariel thought that Nina was her new babysitter. She had no idea that she was dead. She had no questions about what had happened to her, and Nina was glad.

"Is it snack time yet?" So Nina shared her lunch, guiltily wishing that Ariel could stay forever. Well, until Jude got here, of course. The truth was, she was tired of this—of waiting—of everything. She often thought about what it would be like to die together every single time, remembering when Jude asked her to "brainstorm" ways to accomplish this phenomenon. She always reached the same conclusion: there was no way to guarantee it unless they committed suicide together.

When Ariel left, Nina cried and decided that maybe they *should* start committing suicide. The only problem being, of course, that they'd never remember their decision to off themselves once the time came.

She'd never had to wait this long. It'd been 12 years already. This was the first time that she had to watch Jude remarry. She felt horrible for being so heartbroken and restless and impatient…he was the one who waited over 50 years.

Some days, time flew by. Especially when she was in the mood to become her alter ego—motivational speaker Nina. She tried to pull everyone out of their hidden darkest holes, and surprisingly, she was occasionally successful.

Some people still called it "The Recovery Room," but a lot of people were now using the term "The Revival." Others just called it "The Happy." No one called it The Waiting Room anymore. Nina loved that. She loved that it wasn't a "room" anymore. A room is so bland. But The Revival? The Happy? Those sounded like places she'd love to be. They didn't even sound like places, really. More like spiritual points within yourself.

Even more fitting, the new manager was a guru from an ashram in India. The Revival held meditation times daily.

And that's what Jude appeared to—Nina, eyes closed, trying desperately to concentrate on her peace and serenity and all those other things that she supposedly had but could not seem to find. Jude tiptoed around the meditating bodies, trying not to laugh at Nina, who he could see was having a very difficult time.

He bent down slowly and quietly and kissed her neck softly.

"JESUS CHRIST!" she screamed, jumping, and clamping both hands over her mouth.

Giggles filled the un-room-like room.

Joan & Charles

Somehow, we didn't find each other till we were old and worn out. Living in a retirement home, believe it or not.

We both used walkers for goodness sake. And yet, we loved each other like two school children. He wrote me a Valentine card the year I moved in. The writing wasn't very good, but the man could draw beautifully!

I remember thinking my entire life that London was bleak and miserable, even when I was with my husband and children and grandchildren. And then when I met Charles in that spring of 2097, it somehow became the most exciting city in the world.

"Hello, I'm Charles or Chuck or Charlie. And the gardener calls me Cha-Cha. Well, Charles, I prefer Charles." Those were the first words he said. I stuck out my hand and he grabbed it. We didn't shake hands, but rather, held them for a little longer than necessary.

"Hello, Charles. I'm Joan. Pleasure." I smiled up at him (oh my goodness he was so tall). He had this boyish charm about him that took at least 20 years off his life.

I thought about that later that day, after we'd spent all afternoon talking on a bench in the courtyard, when

155

he suddenly exclaimed, "You still have the legs of a 20-something!"

Now *that* made me laugh. I thought he was just trying so hard to compliment me and flirt with me, I thought he'd say anything. But after I noticed how he looked at me, I knew he really meant it. You really can fall in love when you're that age.

And oh, boy, did we fall.

"It would just be downright silly." That's what I kept saying to his marriage proposals.

"Joan, it wouldn't be. I don't want to die a man in love. I want to die a husband to the wife I love." He was pacing back and forth.

I gestured to the photos on my living room wall. My husband of 44 years, who had died from a heart attack. My whole family smiling towards his face.

"They've all met me, Joan, remember? They all loved me!"

"I know, I know. It just seems pointless. I could die to-night in my bed."

He rolled his eyes. We both knew I had much longer than that. I cooked cupcakes for the whole building last week. "Fine, die in your bed alone then." And he walked out, just like that. That had been his 15th proposal. He'd stopped getting down on his knee. It was too hard for him to get back up!

By that point, I knew I never wanted to sleep without his snoring for even one night. I ran outside. He was al-most to his door.

"Fine you old fart! I'll marry you!"

He walked back to me grinning like a fool and said, "How about tomorrow?"

We appeared together, probably both thinking, *I wonder who the new manager is. I wonder what they're calling this place these days. I wonder if there are any more additions to our addition.* This round we'd both been killed in a car accident. Not my fault this time, but a fucking drunk driver. We were so old already though, it didn't really matter. Our cab driver had lived. That probably would've been our last trip into town anyway. We were secretly very glad that we didn't have to plan a hot air balloon ride-gone wrong.

I never got tired of watching Nina's face appear out of someone else's. It was like watching someone I loved more than anything in the world combine with someone else I loved exactly the same amount.

We looked around, sure we were just adjusting, not seeing clearly.

"Where is everybody, baby?" Nina looked up at me, scared.

The room was entirely empty. It looked dusty almost, abandoned.

"I don't know..." Something was very wrong.

And then a tiny, fragile looking, young woman walked out of the break room.

"I thought I heard trouble. Took you two long enough, I've been here for over an hour waiting on your butts. Who would've thought I'd be doing the waiting one day, huh?" I'd never seen this woman in my life, I was sure. Her voice wasn't familiar, but her tone…it couldn't be…

"Ruth?" I picked her up and spun her around. We were both crying and laughing.

"Are you…?" Nina started to ask as she had her turn at a hug.

"Dead? Yes, my dear. Looks like we're the last three dead people to ever exist."

We both eyed her, waiting for an explanation. She waved her hand around the room that was strewn with old handbooks, artwork, stories…

"This is it, kiddos. End of the line."

"I don't understand, Ruthie. Where is everyone?" I sat down next to Nina, who had slumped down in a nearby chair. It was like she already knew. She always seemed to know things before me, sense them. Things were so clear to her. But there I was, in denial. Waiting for Ruth to say, "Just kidding! Gotcha! April Fool's! Everybody's crammed in the break room."

"The Waiting Room is over. The whole process has been cut. To 'simplify'. I'm so sorry." She reached out and put a hand on my shoulder. Nina was crying softly.

"But who got to decide this? Who told you this? It doesn't even make any sense!" Ruth backed a few steps away. I tried to control my breathing, but it was useless. "I SAID, WHO DID THIS?"

She looked at me with sad eyes. "How should I know, Jude? It's just like everything else. You know that."

"No. NO! It can't just…just…end. It's not a fucking person! It can't just die!"

"Everything can die, honey. Remember, I never thought I would. But then I did and it was the best thing that's ever happened to me."

"Well there's no silver fucking lining to this, now is there? Nothing GOOD can come from THIS!"

"You never know what the world will throw at us next. I know it seems like a monstrosity, but what if this is just to make room for something even more brilliant?" Her voice was pleading with me.

"Since when did you become such an optimist?"

"Since I got to live a little myself instead of just watching your ugly mug."

I cracked a smile.

Nina hadn't said one word. She'd walked over to the window. She was clutching a paper in her hand, tears rolling down her cheeks and onto her chest. I touched Ruth's arm, whispered, "Sorry I yelled," and walked over to Nina.

"I wrote this last time, remember?" she whispered.

There once lived a boy named Jude, after the Beatles song, and a girl named Nina, after her great-grandmother, who won best enchiladas in Monterrey 20 years in a row. They weren't anything alike really. They had completely different dreams and completely different ways of working towards those dreams. He liked sports and fast food and politics and he was never on time. He didn't like showering or getting haircuts or going to fancy restaurants. She liked books and school and jewelry and planning. She didn't like scary movies or cigarettes or swimming or snakes. He had a snake. No one ever thought they'd last. But they loved each other without fear or hesitation. And now they meet here, in this room, after every life they spend together, and they wouldn't have it any other way.

"Yeah, I remember," I whispered back, choking up. This couldn't be the last time I'd ever see her and her flowing dark hair, her amazing body hidden underneath the oversized denim dress she'd died in when she was 82.

We held each other for a while and then Nina lifted her head, took my hand, and walked back over to Ruth.

"When did this happen? How long has it been like this?"

"Right after you two left the last time, apparently. A message came through saying that this 'step' has been deemed unnecessary. Now everyone will just begin a new life, without this in-between period."

"So some people weren't even told…" Nina said, almost to herself. She had become some sort of patriot for "the waiters". I'd been trying to think of a title for her, but nothing really summed it up. Each time she waited for me, she spent all her time and energy writing and reading and interviewing. And just talking, getting to know people, sharing our story (even though everyone knew about us by now, of course). She had something positive to say about everything. She remembered every single person she'd ever met, even if it was just a few seconds, teaching them how to dance to Cotton Eyed Joe and then dancing it with them to the door frame. The room was more like a stereotypical "heaven" every time I came here. Except for now, empty. Heaven would never be empty.

"Well, I didn't tell anyone, actually."

Nina looked like she was about to get pissed and start yelling, but then her face softened. "Yeah, I guess that's for the best."

"I guess they didn't want to wait for everyone to die. It would've taken too long. I guess they just wanted to rip it off fast, like a Band-Aid." Ruth's voice was remorseful. Even Ruth could feel Nina's protection of this place, her leadership, her possession, you could almost say.

"You said 'they'."

"It just sounds better than 'It.' I don't even know what to really say. There are a lot of easy words we use that we don't really mean or understand."

"Yeah." Nina hung her head. We all must have been thinking "THIS SUCKS!" Or in Ruth's case, "This is terribly unfortunate."

"There must be someone we can talk to though. This isn't how it ends. You've been receiving these stupid messages for years—someone has to be sending them. That kind of shit doesn't just appear out of thin air!" I punched the back of a chair. Ruth flinched.

"You've never been able to accept that this is just like living on Earth—"

"Because it's not! It's nothing like that!"

"When someone really needs to talk to whatever God or power they believe in, do you think they just appear? No. That's why people pray and worship and read and write and talk to gravestones and do everything else the world does to stay sane!"

"We won't even remember what we've lost anyway," Nina added. "Might as well just watch our grandkids for as long as we can." She started migrating towards the window again.

"But baby, that's the problem! We can't go down without a fight. Since when have you ever gone down without a fight?"

She looked dejected in every way. Even her elbows and eyelashes and knees looked dejected. I wanted to kiss her all over and wake her up, bring her back to my right-hand commander.

"This isn't a fight. This is life and death, the inescapable cycle. Ruth is right. This doesn't mean we'll never see each other again. Who knows what this really means." She reached up and held my face in between her hands. "It's time to let this place go."

Tears started rolling down my cheeks and she brushed them away with her lips.

"Um..." Ruth was looking down at the floor, also crying. What messes we all were. "My name came up."

I wanted to ask her if she'd been the sister of a teenage boy who'd been killed in a school bus accident, but I didn't. Some things are obviously too good to be true.

Nina reached out and held Ruth's hands. They looked at each other and laughed, still crying. "I'm sure we'll see each other again," she whispered, hugging Ruth's tiny frame.

"I'm sure we will, I'm sure we will." They rocked back and forth together.

I guess it's my turn. I couldn't stop crying like a little baby. *This is ridiculous.*

"Ruthie. If I could write you another goodbye letter to read later, once you've forgotten about me, I would. I'd slip it right in your pocket and it'd stay in your crib until you grew up and you were old enough to read it." I hugged her tight.

"Forget you? How could I ever forget you?" She smiled and patted my head and rubbed my back like I was her son. It didn't matter that now she looked 30, her familiar wrinkles mysteriously missing, a stranger's eyes replacing her usual light blues. She was still a mother to me.

Nina watched us walk to the door, hand in hand.

"How does it feel to leave this place, after knowing it for so long?" I felt like I was trembling.

"Like a relief and a heartbreak. All wrapped up in one. I don't know what to think, kind of like the day you tumbled in here." She half-smiled.

I just nodded. "Love you, Ruthie."

"Love you more, kid." Her head didn't even reach my shoulders. She stretched up on her toes and I bent down to let her kiss me swiftly on the cheek. And then she was gone, turning around one last time to give us a little wave before stepping through the door.

CHAPTER 7

Nina was lying across my chest, with nothing but her favorite necklace on. We were sprawled out on the desk. *I wouldn't mind being here, like this, just the two of us, for the rest of time. Maybe our names won't show up.*

"You know, I don't think we should have to make things happen in here. Maybe that's what this is all about. People are supposed to evolve on their own. I was trying so hard to change everyone's next lives, to change the world really, but I guess that wasn't fair." She was stroking my chest hair absentmindedly.

"Maybe. What if after we go through the door, we wake up, and this was all some sick dream? And we're Jude and Nina, in our first and only life, and I never died?"

I pictured it, soaking in the feeling of waking up in our bed, in our house...

"Mmm...that would be perfection."

"Better than being a famous couple?"

"Well I *do* want to be Antony and Cleopatra, Bonnie and Clyde, Lucy and Desi, or oh my God! Pocahontas and John Smith! Or, of course, Romeo and Juliet. I'm tired of living in time periods that are so close together. Let's go Victorian."

"I didn't think Romeo and Juliet were real people."

"Well, it was based on real people."

"Hmm. Bonnie and Clyde would be the best. But aren't they kind of considered to be bad people? Haven't we pretty much established that we're...not...bad people?"

We laughed and kissed and it felt like we were on top of that desk for days.

"I don't think I want to go into present time though," she mused. "Whatever year it really is by now, I'm not sure I want to know what it's like."

"You never know. It could be fantastic. I'd prefer a flying car to a horse, just sayin'. Either way, the sad part is, we won't know what we're missing. I mean, I guess that's a good thing, but still. I feel like we're losing everything—lives, memories, people...it all feels so worthless now." I rolled onto my side and kissed her collarbone.

"I don't think any of it was *worthless*. I think we accomplished *something* here. I have no idea *what* exactly, but *something*."

"Isn't this how reincarnation is supposed to work anyway? You die and you're born, you die and you're born. No creepy waiting-room-in-between-thing."

"I don't know, Hinduism, Buddhism, other ones that I can't remember right now...they're all different and they all get jumbled together in my mind. Isn't it funny though, to think that maybe the 'truth' that people seek is really just a tiny bit of *every* single ideology out there?" She was scratching my scalp and I could feel my eyes getting heavy.

Wouldn't that be hilarious, if we slept through our time?

"So no one's right, no one's wrong?" I mumbled.

"Yeah." She giggled at the thought. "Even agnostics and atheists. Maybe that's just the world's final trick on us."

"Sounds about right." I yawned. "We're just puppets in a giant magic show."

"Don't say that. I don't want to be a puppet."

"But you're not just any puppet, you're the star of the show! You're the most beautiful sock puppet ever created!" She flicked my nipple. "Ouch!" And then we started a brief flicking war. I guess you could say that we've always been the clichéd kids-at-heart type.

"Truce! Truce!" she screamed, jumping off the desk and prancing around. I used to love lounging around the house naked with her. "This is the best part of being married and owning a house," I used to say. Even after this many years, I couldn't' take my eyes off her. This could be our house. God, I wish this was our house.

And then my stomach growled, loudly.

Nina laughed. "I guess we couldn't really survive here, even if we tried. With no one babysitting us," she said, reading my mind. She started putting her clothes on and I reluctantly followed suit.

We watched our family through the "computers" for a while, we kissed like there was no tomorrow (because there wasn't), and we contemplated our fate (99 percent of which was jokes like "I wonder, if I cut off your arm in here, if you'd be born with a stump." Nina's reply to that one was, "I wonder, if I cut off your penis, if you'd be born a girl. Or a hermaphrodite.")

And then, inevitably, a new list printed.

Jude and Nina Floyd. Ten minutes.

Ten minutes to say goodbye forever.

"You know we're not saying goodbye forever, right?" It was almost creepy how she did that sometimes.

"Whatever you say, my love." I buried my head into her neck and my hands into her back and hips and ass and whatever else I could touch.

"Seriously, babe." She pulled away. "We shouldn't be sad. We don't have 'the rest of our life together,' we have the rest of *time* together."

"Honestly? I'd rather have the rest of this day together. Here." I sank into a chair and clutched at her thighs.

"Oh, Jude…"

"In fact, why don't we just stay? What's the worst that could happen? Let's just try it out, yeah?" I was decided. I wasn't budging. Who cares if I never got to live another life? I didn't want to live any more lives, not if I'd never see Nina again, not if I'd ever know about her and us and this.

"No. We can't. You know we can't." She sat down in my lap.

"But why? Why not? We don't even know what will happen. Probably nothing, we'll probably still start another life."

"Probably isn't good enough for me. I'm not taking a chance that I'll never see you again."

"But you *won't* ever see me again! EVER!" I stood up, gently picking her up and putting her on her feet. "Stay with me. Just stay. Please." She gave me a pleading look and I started pacing back and forth. How could I convince her?

"We barely have any time left. C'mon, let's just enjoy this. Let's put on a song. Your turn to pick." She started setting up the ancient CD player, trying to ignore the fact that I wasn't kidding, I was dead (no pun intended) serious.

"Nina. Maybe this is what we were supposed to do all along. Maybe that's why this place is going away, because we didn't follow directions very well, we didn't complete the experiment." I was talking out of my ass, but it actually sounded pretty reasonable.

"Our names came up on the list every single time." Her voice was starting to sound pissed and worried.

"Just because they came up on some stupid list, doesn't mean anything! The list could just be that—a list. A list of people in the room at the time."

"You're the one who told me when I first got here that no one should risk it! You've read what the packet says!"

"But we're not just anyone. And Ruth wrote that, you know that. She has no idea what the truth really is. Let's find out, together."

"Jude Carson Floyd, I will tackle your ass out of here if I have to, you know I will."

Right after she said that, the back wall of the room fell back, silently, letting in a burst of bright light. Papers flew across the room as we shielded our eyes. The wall was simply gone—there was no crash or even a creak. I expected it to be like more of an earthquake or tornado, but the floor beneath us was still, for now.

"See?" Her voice shook. "We'll evaporate into nothingness just like that wall!"

"We'll evaporate into nothingness either way."

One of the side walls gave way. A strong wind flung all of Nina's hair at my face, like it was attacking me.

"No we won't. We've never been nothing. We'll never *be* nothing. We need to hurry, Jude. I'm not leaving without you."

The ceiling started peeling away slowly. Did the room ever really exist at all or were our minds just applying the familiar safety and texture and durability? It seemed to be made out of putty now.

"Well good. I wouldn't leave without you either. Well, again."

Another wall tipped over into the sky. It was like they were running in slow motion. I could still see the ceiling curving away leisurely, like a roller coaster going up, up, up before a huge drop.

"You know what, no! I'm not going to risk never being able to live again, and I can't believe you'd even want me to risk that! Do you hear yourself? I guess I won't be living with you by my side anymore, but I'm going." She started to walk towards the door, turned back and gripped my arms. "Please. Please! Come with me! Do this for me! Stop being a complete idiot! Look around! This place is literally falling into a black hole! Never go down without a fight, remember? Find a way to die together, remember? Let's do this! Let's fight! Let's die! Let's do *something* other than stand here until we disappear or melt or dissolve!"

169

Her eyes were so, so much more green than brown when she cried. That was always the first thing I thought when I saw her start to tear up. The last wall floated away, effortlessly. We were surrounded by light. *This is more like the Heaven people picture. If only we were on a cloud.* Chairs began to be swept away quietly. Everything was so quiet. Nothing like the natural disaster that I thought it was. It was closer to a ballet without the music. I wondered if it was too late to choose a CD.

"Ok." I wiped her cheeks and kissed her.

"Ok?"

"Ok." I nodded. Who was I kidding? I could hardly ever say no to this woman. And after a speech like that, I wasn't even going to try.

The floor began to strip downwards from the far right-hand corner and we ran to the door, stopping quickly at the last square of tile for one last kiss.

"I love you so much." She was smiling, with the most hopeful glint that I'd ever seen in her eyes.

"I'll see you soon." I kissed her again and we walked through, as I resisted the urge to say, "Goodbye."

Abigail & Edward

I met him in the kitchen in 1755, but I'd seen him long before that. I don't think he ever really saw me, but he sure did that day. I walked in covered head to toe in mud, cryin' like a child. He was perched up on the counter, sneakin' pie out off the windowsill. We both jumped at the sight of each other and laughed nervously.

"Sorry sir," I said, trying to control my tears. "Should I come back later?"

"You can call me Edward. And I reckon' you better stay and get cleaned up. I'll go."

"You don't have to." He looked at me funny and I blushed. "I mean, I'm just gonna wash my face right quick." He looked me over, probably realizing that this was the only dress I owned. I was one of the only white maids left in probably the whole state of Alabama. Everybody had slaves now, for less than half the price. But Mr. and Mrs. Jackson kept Mama on and even let me come work too, last year. People around town sometimes called us "those light-skinned niggers."

"You fall?"

"Yessir."

"How?" He took another big bite of pie.

I blushed again. "I was chasin' the cat."

He laughed loudly and I quickly looked around. I'd get skinned alive if I was caught not only talkin' to him, but talkin' to him with mud all over me.

"Who, you mean old Whiskers?"

"Yessir. I love him." I looked at my brown-covered shoes. Did I just say that I loved his cat? Oh Lord help me.

"You don't have to call me sir, you know. I'm probably not even older than you."

I eyed him silently, walking over to the faucet. I'd never been this close to him. "Yes you are. You're 16, I'm 14."

"How'd you know that?" He jumped off the counter and now he was right up next to me, inches away, pie crumbs lining his mouth. He smelled like apples and dirt and sweat. I probably smelled like mud.

"Mama's worked here since you were born," I whispered, wiping my face slowly with my wet fingers.

"Oh yeah. I forget she's your mama sometimes."

"I know, she don't act like it is why."

"Oh." And then he did the strangest thing. He picked a flake of mud outa my hair, just like that, like we'd been best friends forever or somethin'.

I called him Edward after that, but only when we were alone.

Cara & Zak

Online dating? Had I really stooped this low? The answer was yes, yes I had. Sure, it was normal these days. Over half of the population met via instant messaging. But since when had I ever wanted to be part of the majority? Besides, there was something so...icky about it. Call me strange, but I like to see a man's face when I say something that ruins the conversation and makes him yearn for the check.

I created the stupid little profile, uploading a 5-year old picture, of course. Damn, I looked so much better when I was 35. I took what seemed like a thousand personality and compatibility tests. Now all that was left was my "tagline."

I seriously considered typing "Crazy Workaholic Divorced Female" as my overall description, but decided to be a little less honest. Also considered were: "Divorced, no kids, hardly any friends, no life" and "Sad, lonely, and pathetic. But quite well-off and well-traveled" and "No green thumb, hates pets, hasn't had sex in four years, but willing to try all three. Except the plants thing. Fuck that."

The winner-winner-chicken-dinner was "Fashion Magazine Editor, loves to cook and travel, looking for someone to laugh with." How clichéd could I get? But it was so true. I'd be perfectly happy never finding love again (if you can call what me and my ex-husband had love), if I just had someone that made me smile.

I surfed through the profiles that supposedly "matched me perfectly." Boring, boring, ugly, extremely ugly, extremely obese, six kids (hell to the no), completely bald (I just don't think I could do it), 20 years older than me, 30 years older than me, and a ginger. I usually don't go for redheads. What great options. I almost escaped as quickly as physically possible, but then I realized, who am I to be picky? I scrolled through my options again. The ginger was actually really handsome, especially when I covered up his hair with my pointer finger. I liked his bio a lot too. "Architect, Divorced, one daughter. Don't pick me just because I can build you a beautiful house. Yes, people have dated me for this reason." I read that a few times, smiling, and squinting about an inch away from the monitor to try and see his dimples more clearly. Zak Hammond. That was a great name.

A green light suddenly came on next to his smile. "Online. Chat?" it asked.

"Oh, what the hell," I said out loud, taking a swig of

Dr. Pepper.

"Hi." I was original.

"Hello. Your ears must have been burning."

"Should I be creeped out by that statement?" I already didn't like this situation. Not being able to hear his voice. Voices and tones and inflections and accents…it's all very important stuff if you ask me. He could type like a professor and speak like a crack dealer. You never know.

"Haha, no. I got a message with your profile embedded in it, says that you're a new match." Oh, good Lord, I was going to need something stronger than a Dr. Pepper. I poured a glass of wine and sat back down. Did this guy really believe that a few tests could prove that we would work together?

"So who were you talking to about me?"

"What do you mean?"

"You said my ears must have been burning."

"Oh, haha." I was glad he didn't use "Lol". I hated that shit. People don't actually laugh out loud unless it's laugh-out-loud-able. "I guess I misused that expression. My own thoughts about you and your profile don't cause ears to burn I guess." His thoughts about me? That sounded dirty. I don't know if I can do this.

"So what were you thinking?"

I sensed a slight hesitation in his typing. He'd responded to everything else so quickly. "I was thinking that you sound like a very interesting and ambitious woman. I'd like to know more."

For the next five and a half hours, we basically told our life stories. My fingers felt like they were about to fall off. I liked everything about him though. I never knew you could be so attracted to someone's personality simply through online chatting. It was ridiculous how much I wanted to talk to him over the phone or in person. I hadn't given the "ginger thing" a second thought. The wine didn't help.

I closed my eyes and said a silent prayer that I wasn't about to make a HUGE mistake.

"Maybe we should talk on the phone sometime?"

"I would love that. Are you going to bed anytime soon?" It was 11:30 on a Saturday night. Usually, the answer would've been, "Yes, my bedtime was three hours ago." I lived dangerously on the weekends. He obviously didn't do much on Saturday nights either though. We were in the same time zone, thank God.

"Um, not sure. You?"

"Well, I know it's late, and I know we've already talked all night…but could I call you right now?"

My stomach flipped and I suddenly wondered what I looked like, frantically imagining my wrinkly yoga jumpsuit, no make-up, and messy ponytail. Also, I probably looked drunk by now. Mainly because I *was* drunk.

It was like he read my mind: "We don't have to video. We can just talk the old-fashioned way." I could've kissed the computer screen.

"Ok. Sounds good."

Kapio & Zavi

Kapiolani had dreams of escaping The House of Bottles. All the dreams were different, but one thing always stayed the same—she never cut her feet. She'd run and run and run, through all the rooms, over all the bottles, and her legs would just bounce off the colored glass gracefully. Her toes were unscathed, her heels smooth and soft, her arches still white frowns against the floor.

The way she felt in the dream was the way she felt when she was dancing hula. The sway of her hips and wave-like motions of her arms reminded her of the way she looked in the dreams—so much like her mother. Or at least like the pictures she had seen. There was one in the living room with writing scrawled all over her mother's body; the only piece not touching the faded black marker was her eyes. "Tanu," it said, and then a fancy scribbling of Hawaiian words that Kapiolani pretended to know, "-Kainoa."

Kapiolani would make up thousands of sentences that her mother could be writing to her father all over the pink bikini and brown skin. "I love you" or "I miss you" or "I want to have a beautiful daughter with you" or, her favorite, "I will never leave you. I will always return." She never asked her dad what the message really said because she didn't want to know. She would see her father staring at it sometimes though, and she'd want more than ever to leave the hall, run up to him, place her hand on his unshaven cheek, and ask the millions of questions she'd built up over the years. What was she like? Do I look like her? What did her voice sound like? What did she smell like? Could she cook? Could she hula? And what, please, what does the photograph say?

But then she'd see him take another swig of his drink or

hear him curse something at the television and Kapiolani would shrink away, back into the hall, back into her room, away from the bottles and into the same dream.

Tonight, she fell asleep with her feet where her head usually lay. She did that sometimes when sleep seemed farther away than the mainland. Her dad had those friends over again and they were laughing beer-filled laughs and coughing up smoke and spit. She could never sleep when they were over, clinking ice and eating her lunch that she'd packed and hidden in the back of the fridge.

"Wea dat pretty daughtah, eh, Tanu?" Grunts and snorts and more glass hitting glass would follow and Kapiolani would lock her door. She learned a long time ago to do that. She never forgot.

A taped-together photo of her mother rested gingerly beneath her pillow. It had been rescued from the trash after Tanu had gone on a ripping rampage one night. He never touched the framed one in the living room, but this one was Kapiolani's second favorite. It used to be under a magnet on the freezer. Her mother, lips red like ahi, was kissing a tiny, tiny forehead that held a tiny, tiny red like ahi headband. These two, this mother and daughter, they looked magical, Kapio thought. They looked unstoppable together. Like ancient Hawaiian royalty or something.

Eventually, maybe after a short, whispered conversation with the photograph, she'd fall asleep. Tonight, she waited until she heard the heavy drunken footsteps leave The House of Bottles. Her mind was almost lost in the dream when, "KAPIO! WEA YOU AT?" jolted her up to a sitting position. The picture fell from her chest to the floor. BOOMBOOMBOOM, the door shook and she could feel her body start to do the same.

An image plastered itself to every inch of her mind: graceful, smiling, hula hipped, red lipped, escape.

BOOMBOOMBOOM!

Her face, her mother's face, she couldn't tell which one it was, but it snuck out through the window. She wasn't dreaming, but it felt the same as she followed in the footsteps of the image and slid the screen open slowly.

BOOMBOOMBOOM! "YOU BETTAH OPEN DIS DOOR!"

She grabbed the photo and the 43 dollars that she hid every day in the pages of her math book, shoving them into her backpack and dropping it out the window, climbing quickly after it.

BOOMBOOMBOOM! The banging was a little bit quieter as her feet hit glass. She hadn't even thought to put on pants or shoes. You're an idiot, she thought, only in your stupid dream are your feet protected. Now, as her soft skin touched the shards that covered their backyard, she had no choice. If she wanted to escape, this was the only way. Kapio planted both feet firmly, feeling small flakes and large chunks rip into her flesh with ease. And she ran. Across the lawn that had served as years' worth of ash trays and garbage cans, away from The House of Bottles, so far away that she could stop and catch her breath and pick out some stubborn pieces from her heels and toes, looking back on the sidewalk to see little specks of blood.

She smiled. She laughed, looking down at her cotton

panties and skinny knees. She had actually reenacted the dream instead of just thinking, wishing, hoping, dreaming of the dream. She was so elated that the pain felt like success. Her auntie's house was only a few more blocks, and even though she knew it'd be the first place he'd come BOOMBOOMBOOMing, she also knew that he was too drunk to do anything this late at night. He'd just break down her bedroom door, see that she'd run away, and pass out in her bed. Or he'd be too tired for that and simply pass out in front of the door, head slumped against the handle, drool covering his stubble, and a bottle leaning into his crotch. She'd found him like this a few times, and had to gently lay his body out in the hall so she could step over it and catch the bus. It was the morning that loomed ahead.

It was the morning that Kapio would have to clean her feet with peroxide and bandage them up and borrow clothes from her cousin and go to school, holding her breath, expecting him to show up in every classroom. It was the morning that she'd have to escape all over again and it was the morning that she'd realize escaping is impossible. It was the morning that she'd understand what dreams are for. Dreams are for impossibilities, delights, unrealistic ambitions. Dreams are for mothers coming home and fathers being sober.

Dreams are for hula dancing over bottles, skin untouched, lips red like ahi.

That is, until she met the cutest haole at Campbell High School. He came from THE House of Bottles and his name was more complicated than any local kine boy. Xavier but everyone called him "Zavi". Kapio thought that was the weirdest thing ever. But his hair was like sunshine and his eyes were like Lanikai waters and his smile was only for her and he was from THE House of Bottles.

"I dreamt of you," he said, studying her everything.

"I dreamt of escape."

"That's what I meant. That's what we're gonna do."

And they did.

Alondra & Rosalio

sleepytime tea and a one
bedroom apartment
my life is suddenly so still
I like it sometimes—
so quiet I can hear this pen's marks,
my breath,
faint footsteps of the neighbor
it's peaceful and calm
and who am I kidding
the reason I'm so at ease,
so comfortable, so familiar
is because this life is lonely
it's actually a shocking realization—
that I've been lonely all my life
that's why this feels OK
that's why I'm content
listening to the dryer's hum
I've been lonely ever since I
can remember
-a

The Waiting Room

you left my body outlined in chalk/you didn't even make
time to talk
you left the yellow tape rolled out/it
was too late to scream or shout

you walked away /I didn't and did
want you to stay
I gasped for air/I didn't and did want you to care

you didn't look back/I bled on the concrete/you didn't
even crack/that's what I call a defeat
I watched your shoes disappear/Halloween nightmare/or
metaphorical fear?
Rosalio

I wait for you in bad decisions,
bad haircuts, and bad drunken poetry.
I wait for you in difference parts of the world
I wait for you everywhere I go.
they always say you'll come when I stop waiting
maybe that's my problem
because I'll always be waiting:
behind grocery store carts
sweating makeup drops at the gym
every chair I've ever sipped coffee in
every man I meet, every man I kiss
I'm waiting
I wait for you in brand new dresses
at lonely bars and restaurants
I wait for you through cheap sunglasses

and 30 spf on lonelier beaches
whoever you are, wherever you are
I just thought I'd wait to say
that I'm so tired of waiting
but I can't seem to stop
maybe if you just come around,
show your face
then I can wait on your call
instead of your introduction
what do you say?
-a

> I'm getting there/I'm getting there
> my teeth are showing more each day/it's
> about to be a new year

> and I'm ready, I'm so ready/hand
> over that clean slate
> bring on the good things, no the
> great/I want to open this and

> be happy to keep writing/to see etchings
> of smiles and love
> do people have time?/ to write poetry
> when they're living that life?
> Rosalio

I want you like buttered toast
always, all times of day
I want you like belief
of which I have none.
I want you like love

of which I've had little
I want you like
things that are too expensive
places that are too far away
and dreams that are too unrealistic
I far-fetch want you
I dream-big want you
I high-hopes want you
I buttered toast want you
-a

                    lovely unfolding of persona and tongue/I
                    ravish you and your thoughts unshared
            with the average man in your bed/irresistible overlap-
                            ping of memory and spit

                        I kiss your presence—neck and aura,
                        shoulder and soul/it's all wrapped up,
                        messy, like my torn apart sheets

            physical and emotional, sex and friendship/orgasms
                                    and trust
            I had forgotten how it all swirls/but I think maybe it
                            never swirled like this before
                                    Rosalio

She loved him in handfuls, like dirt offerings from a toddler
She kissed him in scoops, like his favorite: vanilla swiss
    almond
She loved him in buckets—like sand to build their dream
    home, concrete to build the real one

She kissed him in gallops and leaps, like running in the
airport
She loved him in spoonfuls and mouthfuls and fistfuls
She loved him in every way, in every room, in every season,
of every year
But most of all, she loved him without fear.
-a

it turns out you do have time/when both of you have
the same pen to paper disease
the blood of ink before bed/when most are flipping
through channels

we sit and we jot down stanzas/so today I will brain-
storm for the latest, I know I will write
Marry me, amor? at the bottom/and I will pass her the
poem like I so often do

but this time I'll set a ring on top/and this time she
won't just nod and kiss me
she won't just give me a silly alliteration compliment/
this time she'll write back, or maybe not

either way, I know she'll say yes/yes to being mine and
me hers and this ours
because after all/it's always been ours
it feels like
Rosalio

Vi & Blaine

I first saw her face on a playbill, and I just thought, *God, I gotta have her*. I liked everything about her three-sentence bio that said she was from Nevada but she was born in France. And the tiny black and white picture, where she was smiling without teeth, so cautiously. I never once have told her that, she'd laugh right in my face or kick me with her red stilettos she wears all the time.

Therefore, she'll never know that I didn't just *happen* to be in the coffee shop that I knew she went to every night after the show. She'd dump me in a heartbeat and never look back once.

"This is 2555. The divorce rate is 85 percent. Marriage and relationships and love in general are slowly becoming jokes. Worthless, pathetic pastimes that people still have some bizarre attraction to. So don't go thinking this is anything more than coffee, k?"

I'd sat there, a little shocked, but still desperately hoping I could change her mind. She was absolutely radiant, still in stage makeup and a slinky black dress.

"So, uh, what do you do? I'm Blaine, by the way, I work the lights over at The Majestic."

She eyed me suspiciously. "I just started working at The Majestic. You've never seen me?"

"Oh, really?" I was *not* a good actor, and she could tell. "I, uh, only work the early shifts."

She smiled knowingly. But at least she didn't know that I followed her here. And at least she didn't call me out for lying. "Well I'm a singer, trying to act, basically. If you want to call it that." She laughed darkly. "The Majestic isn't exactly Broadway, as I'm sure you know. And I'm definitely not a lead."

"That's so great though, you're doing what you love."

She laughed darkly again and took a sip of her even darker coffee. "Who said I loved it?"

"You don't?" I was incredulous. She was so talented! (She also never knew that I'd seen her perform before).

She took another sip and played with her spoon. "I mean, I guess I do, yeah. I just feel like it's an insignificant art nowadays. No one cares. The theaters aren't ever full anymore. I see all these pictures and videos of how it used to be and I think, why wasn't I alive *then*, when it actually meant something?"

"A lot of people still care. I still care."

"Everything beautiful dies." I wasn't sure if she'd even heard me. "Everything that I care about, I mean. Libraries? I loved them. And dollar bills. I know it's stupid, but I miss all things paper. And did you know they're closing down this coffee shop? It's been my favorite for years." She motioned around the room. There was one other person sitting, drinking a latte. "This was one thing I thought would never go out of style. Wrong again."

She was so bitter, full of hate. Her insides and outsides don't match up, I mused.

"Were you here in '39 when there was that huge protest at the old library?"

"I was there."

"Me too." I tested out a smile, feeling like every word I said and every emotion I unveiled was like walking on eggshells. I wanted her to like me so badly. I could work on making her love me later, if she just liked me now, in this one moment.

"Please don't tell me you were one of those lunatics shouting 'Save our trees! Save our Earth!'" In a mere two decades, the country had become 100 percent paperless. Everything was sold or recycled or burned or donated. No one really cared, but my parents were disgraced.

I laughed. "No, not me. My mother was a librarian, actually. One of the last of her kind, she always says. I was there trying to stop her from murdering those people."

We both laughed this time. How amazing it was to see her teeth behind that lipstick.

"She sounds like a great woman."

"Yeah, she's a riot." I eyed her, trying to decide if she was worth it, even though I already knew the answer. "Here, I have a present for you."

"Ooh, a present from a guy I've known for five whole minutes? Must be my lucky day." She smirked and her eyes bore into me. She wasn't fiddling with her coffee or glancing around the room, I finally had her attention.

I opened my wallet and crumpled the dollar bill into my palm. I'd been carrying it around since I was six, when they started to slowly weed out paper money entirely. My mom had told me, "Let it remind you of simplicity. Life can still be like that if you let it. Oh, and don't let anybody see it!"

"For you." I closed my palm around hers, letting the worn, faded, extinct object pass from my hand into hers.

She gasped. "No way," she whispered in awe. "You can't give me this!"

"I just did." I smiled broadly. "I've been carrying it around too long, it's someone else's turn."

Her eyes darted around. "Isn't it illegal?" She closed her hand into a fist and held it against her chest. In a flash, her hard exterior had cracked and I could see who she really was, leaning across the table towards me, a curl falling in front of her face.

"My family doesn't pay much attention to the law, you could say." I laughed at how that sounded. "I mean, we're not criminals or anything." I laughed again, nervously this time. I can't tell you enough how beautiful and confident she looked—she looked like a goddamn movie star smack in the middle of a drab, hole-in-the-wall coffee shop.

"Well then what did you mean?" She was still clutching the dollar as if any moment, it would fly away.

"We helped my mom steal 350 books before they were sold to Mexico. All our favorites or ones we'd been meaning to read. My dad tried to tell her she could still read them, that books weren't being outlawed, just paper books. She didn't care. She says it's not the same. In school, all the other kids used to make fun of me because she'd make me take the paper versions of everything. She said I'd learn better. I got suspended four times because of it. You should come with me sometime; my parents' basement is probably the world's last library." I suddenly felt like I'd been talking for ages. I blushed, clearing my throat.

She reached out and put her hand on mine. "I would absolutely love to. Is it too late tonight?"

And there was that instant—that weird, bizarre, crazy

second where you think to yourself, *This is who I want to spend the rest of my life with.*

Jude looked around, extremely confused. This wasn't The Waiting Room, or whatever the hell they were calling it last time he checked.

This was new, this was very new.

This is different. He smiled and didn't know whether to cry or laugh or both.

And then, naturally, he waited.

Made in the USA
Lexington, KY
04 September 2016